CHRISTINA GREEN

THE MAGIC OF THORN HOUSE

Complete and Unabridged

LINFORD
Leicester

First published in Great Britain in 2016

First Linford Edition
published 2017

A catalogue record for this book is available
from the British Library.

ISBN 978–1–4448–3256–3

Published by
F. A. Thorpe (Publishing)
Anstey, Leicestershire

Set by Words & Graphics Ltd.
Anstey, Leicestershire
Printed and bound in Great Britain by
T. J. International Ltd., Padstow, Cornwall

This book is printed on acid-free paper

1

I stood by the gate and stared. This was Aunt Jem's famous old home, where I had spent my childhood. Well, it looked a bit the worse for wear now, I thought. She had raved about the Tudor chimneys, the ancient windows with their bottle glass, and above all the warm welcome that hit you the moment you opened that enormous black oak front door.

'Carla, love,' she had said from her bed where she lay, coping with the heart disease that was taking its toll on her, 'remember that it is historic, full of the stories of people who have lived there in the past. Allow your mind to wander, and you will see what I mean.'

Now, bravely, I stepped up to the door and found the huge iron key that would open this wonderland — willed to me by dear Aunt Jem, who died some four months ago, and now my property — and wondered what I should find indoors. The key scraped and needed a firm twist, the door squeaked as it slowly opened, and then two steps, and I was inside.

I stood quite still, breathing deeply, and aware of something very strange — something warm holding together the musty smells, and the distant creaking of a timber somewhere in the house, the warmth making this a pleasant moment as I remembered the past. It was as if Aunt Jem's old house was welcoming me back again.

I felt all the nervous tension that had held me together as I drove down from London this morning fading away. I walked further into the shadowy hall and looked up a dark wooden staircase. 'Hallo,' I said aloud, and heard my voice ring through the distant rooms, upstairs and down. Almost as if the house were waiting for me; yes, welcoming me. I thought I would reply, telling it what to expect now I, the new owner, had arrived.

'Don't worry about anything,' I said, smiling. 'I'll get you back into good shape and then we'll all be happy here. All of us who used to be here — and anyone I invite to come and stay. I'm Carla, Carla Marshall — do you remember me? — and I'm loving coming back here. Now, can I start seeing how you are?' And I took my first step up the creaking wooden staircase.

But before I reached the top, a croaky voice down in the hallway called to me. 'Well, look who it is! Carla, come back to the old house. We've been waiting for you to arrive. Wait, I'll come up with you.'

And suddenly there was this old woman at my side. She grinned, pounded her chest to relieve her breathlessness, and swung her arm around mine. 'Help me up this last bit, there's a good maid. See, I'm asthmatic; makes me puff coming in here with all the dust and these uneven stairs. Annie Grey — remember me? So you've come back from London, have you?'

I helped her up the remaining few steps until we stood together at the head of the stairway. Then I smiled at her. 'Of course

I remember you.' Just that she had got older, I thought.

She looked at me curiously with her faded but keen eyes. 'Going to live here, are you, maid? Or just turn it into flats and bring all the posh city people down here?'

I felt my thoughts running in circles. I wasn't sure what the answer to her straightforward question might be. Yes, I had wondered about doing the old house up and then living here for a bit — just a short holiday, really, before going back to London and continuing my work there. But making it into flats and having all sorts of strangers taking over the old place? Suddenly I knew I wasn't going to do that.

'No,' I said firmly. 'No strangers in flats. Just me, cleaning everything up and enjoying being in the country again. And then, well, I'm not sure … '

Annie pushed her old mouth into a grimace. She said very certainly, 'Once you'm here you won't want to leave. Thorn House does that, you see. It puts a spell on you. So if you're not sure 'bout living here, go now. I'm telling you, Thorn makes people stay forever.'

I managed a laugh. This was all nonsense — old folks' tales that I vaguely remembered being told me; and Annie was probably full of them. 'I'll let you know later what my plans are. At the moment I'm keen to see what the house is like now. I'll just go along this passage ... '

Together we wandered from room to room, with Annie reminding me of the past. 'This is where Miss Jem slept — morning sun, and then she went into the room on the other side of the passage for her afternoon rest. See that cosy old armchair? I can see her there now, waiting for her tea. She had her old maid, Bertha, with her from years ago, and they were as thick as thieves. Bertha cooked and shopped and did a bit of dusting while Miss Jem listened to her stories and wrote some of them down. A book writer, she was.'

'Yes,' I said, looking around the prettily decorated bedroom. 'I know she was. I've got all her books. They'll move in, with me.'

Annie's grimace softened into a grin. 'Well, if you wants help, I'm only down the road. Rose Cottage, that's me.'

We looked into each other's eyes and I felt her warmth. Yes, she was the same nosey old woman that I remembered, but she had known Aunt Jem, and she knew all about Thorn House.

We moved along the passage to find another dusty bedroom at the end of the corridor. After a bit more wandering around the rooms — all of them dusty, all in good need of a fresh look — I thought that was enough. And I was reminded about the thorn tree.

'I know it's called Thorn House, Annie — and I saw the thorn tree is still there,' I said conversationally as we walked back down the stairs.

Her face stretched into an amused but secretive smile. 'When you go into the garden you'll see it again, maid. Huge old May tree stretches all over the wall — the old people here called it the thorn tree, so the house got that name. Could tell you a few stories about that May tree, I could.'

That was the hawthorn, the wonderful flowering native tree that came out in bloom in the month it was named after, and then had bright red haws in the autumn. Yes, and thorns all over its stems.

I remembered Annie's tales. Again we looked at each other, and I understood that if, as I was planning, I came to spend some time here, Annie Grey could do more than tell me a few old tales. She could be a real helper in my new countrified life.

Suddenly I wanted to see it again, to remind myself. I locked up the house, put the key in my pocket, and said, 'Right, let's go and look at our famous old tree then, Annie.'

She stood quite still, grinning at me and pointing at a huge bush that stood at the corner of the house, its greenery quite concealing the edges of the stone wall. It was very big and wild now, and I wondered that Aunt Jem hadn't ordered it to be pruned every so often. I knew she liked her garden to be neat and tidy, but this hawthorn seemed to have taken over for several years. It was imposing, and attractive in a wild way. I walked up to it, felt the thorns, looked into its thick leaves and saw small buds forming. Well, it was late April now, and May would be here quite soon. And clearly the hawthorn — the thorn tree — would be in flower in a few weeks.

A strange little burst of excitement hit me. My old house, my thorn tree, and it would soon be spreading its wild, fragrant flowers all over the far wall, where a path led to the back garden. I found myself following that path, rough and stony and hard on my city-clad feet. I needed to see where the thorn tree was leading me.

Behind me, I heard Annie say, 'Gotta go home now and make the tea. Come and see me if I can help in any way, maid. Cheerio fer now … ' And I knew I was alone. Alone in what opened out to be a big, sloping garden with a huge hedge bank at the far end, with great trees growing out of it. Halfway up the

THE MAGIC OF
THORN HOUSE

After the death of her dear Aunt
Jem, Carla Marshall inherits Thorn
House, the ancient country manor
where she spent a happy childhood.
But her arrival brings with it fresh
problems. She meets and falls in
love with local bookseller Dan
Eastern — but is he only after the
long-lost manuscript of one of Aunt
Jem's books, which would net him a
fortune if Carla can find it? And her
aunt's Memory Box hides a secret
that's about to turn Carla's world
upside down . . .

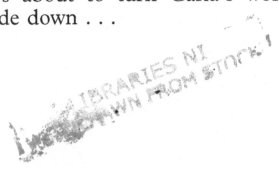

Books by Christina Green
in the Linford Romance Library:

VILLAGE OF WHISPERS
WOODSMOKE
WILD ENCHANTMENT
TIDE OF UNCERTAINTY
SHELTER FROM THE STORM
ROBYN LEE
THE LOVING HEART
TRUST IN ME
LUCY OF LARKHILL
RACHEL'S FLOWERS

rough grass I stopped and looked at them. An immensely tall oak, an even bigger ash tree, and smaller trees dotted the hedge that enclosed the garden. Hazel, I guessed, and perhaps even damson, for Aunt Jem had made wonderful damson jam, I remembered.

Standing there, surrounded by this wild garden, I found my thoughts racing around my bewildered mind. This was mine, all mine — what was I going to do with it? I had a good job in London and a small, comfortable apartment which, until recently, I had shared with Alan, now my ex-partner. We had amicably decided that our separate jobs were too busy to allow us to be together sufficiently to carry on our three-year-old relationship. Was I going to shut up the old house, return to London and its chaotic, noisy life, and rent this place out to someone else who would keep it going for a few more years?

What a dilemma. I moved now, approaching the thick hedge and wondering if birds nested there, if acorns still fell from the oak tree, and if those flying seeds that I remembered came from ash trees, scattering the ground in the autumn.

I walked slowly, fingering here a leaf, then looking for the grasshopper I heard in the grass around my feet. The rough path I followed led up beside the hedge bank and then diverted through a small rickety gate. I pushed through, finding myself on a small patch of rough ground, mostly long grass and a few wildflowers. But what caught my eye at once was a long strip of newly dug soil. Beside it, a fork stood upright next to a row of small flowerpots with seedlings growing in them. And then at the end of the row, I spotted some tall plants that I recognised as beans of some sort, growing up bamboo canes and forming an obelisk around them.

Memories of Aunt Jem's ancient gardener, Mr Bowles, came flying back into my mind. Mr Bowles, despite his unwillingness to share his provender, had been an excellent gardener. Many years ago, of course. But now it was quite clear that somebody else was trying to restore the old vegetable patch.

I wandered back through the gate and made my way towards the garden shed, just visible beyond the border of shrubs, with ivy growing all over it. Approaching, I saw that the door was open and someone was standing over a shelf, cleaning a small tool, unaware that I was here.

I took a deep breath, wondering who this uninvited gardener was, and hoping that he wouldn't react too strongly when I appeared.

2

The teenage boy standing there almost dropped the tool he was working on, and I saw it was a garden trowel he was cleaning until it sparkled. I stepped up to the door and said, 'Hallo — who are you?'

He turned to face me, and stared, and I thought I recognised anxiety on his young face. But there was also a radiance in his blue eyes, and a determined set to his mouth. For a moment he didn't speak, so I smiled firmly and said, 'Cat got your tongue? I'm Carla Marshall, the new owner of this old house — and it looks as if you're my new gardener. So tell me ... '

He wasn't tall, but stocky with strong shoulders. His clothes were shabby, but fitted him and looked right. He moved away from the shelf, pushed up a folding chair, and said, 'Want to sit down, do you?'

I shook my head, and suggested we go into the house to make a drink of some sort. Instead, he reached to the floor, where a flask stood beside his backpack. 'Coffee,' he said, with not quite a grin. 'Enough for two, I should think.'

'Great. Tell me your name, and let's go get some mugs, shall we?' I led the way onto the path and down to the back door of the house with him following, carrying both his backpack and the flask of coffee.

'Jake Woodley,' he said as we walked. 'I know I shouldn't be here, but everyone said the house was empty and the garden gone wild, and I thought, well, here's my chance to grow things. Vegetables, I thought. Which I could sell. I've been trying to get an allotment, but they're all taken these days. So I came here. But you're here now, so, of course ... '

We went into the house to the kitchen, where chairs stood around the long scrubbed table. I sat down and nodded at him. 'I'll find some mugs. Sit down and we'll talk. And don't worry about me being here — we can probably work out something if you really want to do the work.'

I wasn't at all sure of what I was saying. Did I truly want a teenager with heavy shoulders around my garden? Wouldn't it be wiser to tell him 'Sorry, but you must go'? But he pushed my mug of coffee towards me, and I saw disappointment tighten up his face.

'I do,' he said simply. 'I love gardening. I want to make things grow as well as I can. And I can't do it at home, you see.'

I sipped my coffee. A bit weak, and too sweet, but it wasn't bad. 'Why not?' I asked.

He was quiet for a moment, and I guessed he was trying to decide how much to tell me.

Carefully I asked, 'Still at school, are you?'

At once he frowned and came to life. 'No. Walked out. Had enough of it — but of course Kev got at me, didn't he?'

I drank some more coffee. 'Who's Kev?'

Looking at me with an expression of extreme displeasure, he muttered, 'My brother, Kevin. Older than me. Works hard all day. He's a builder; wants me to do the same. Or filling shelves in a supermarket, or working for him — all that stuff. I said no. I'm going to do what I want, and he doesn't like that.' A long pause, and then, 'We don't get on.'

I felt myself becoming drawn in and wished the boy hadn't been here at the same time as me. But something was pushing me on. Surely Jake needed some sort of help? And as I was here, perhaps I was the one who could offer it. 'Where do you live, Jake?' I asked him.

He looked across at me, and I thought I saw hope in his lean young face. 'With Kev,' he said. 'In town.' I watched his thoughts running. 'Our mum died last year, and we never had a dad. Sort of hard, really.'

I nodded. 'I'm sorry about that. But this idea of growing things — tell me about it.'

The tension faded from his face. 'Yeah,

I love it. I've always wanted to have a garden. Mum used to grow things, and we ate all the veg she grew. But Kev's too busy with work to do anything like that, so I thought I'd start my own little business, growing and then selling. Everyone's into fresh veg today, aren't they? I could do really well.'

Now he was half-smiling, and I understood that I couldn't step away from this enthusiasm and need. And anyway, my new garden needed someone working on it. I thought hard for a moment, then said, 'I'll let you do what you want with that top bit of rough land, but I need something in return. No, not money, but perhaps a bit of work in the rest of the garden. What d'you say?'

Such a smile, and I knew I was doing the right thing. And if he turned out to be a confused lad just looking for kicks and running wild, I'd boot him out. But somehow I found myself thinking that Jake Woodley was a young man who saw his way ahead, and was determined to go further down the path to running a small business.

I didn't have to wait long for his answer. Grinning, he said, 'I'll do it. Whatever you want. If you'll just let me go on growing my veg up there ... Thanks, Miss Marshall. Wow, when I tell Kev he'll jump about a bit, but he's got to understand it's I want to do.'

The coffee was finished. He put the empty flask into the backpack on the floor, stood up, and flashed me another amazing grin. 'You won't be sorry,' he said. 'Promise. I'd better go and finish what I was doing before I go home. But I'll be here tomorrow.' In the doorway he turned and looked at me. 'Not having me on, are you? 'Cause, well, it's almost too good to be true.'

I got up, walked to his side, and put my arm on his shoulder. 'As long as you're straight with me, Jake, I'll be the same with you. Now go home and tell your brother what's happening.'

His grin died and he frowned. 'Can't imagine what Kev'll say.'

Without any thought, I said, 'If he's

difficult, ask him to come here and see me, and I'll explain. OK?'

I could see him thinking, feeling anxious, and yet hoping. Eventually he nodded and went on his way back to the garden shed, but he gave me a last grin. 'OK, Miss Marshall. See you tomorrow, then. Cheers.' And he disappeared from view.

I went back to the kitchen, put the mugs in the sink, and sat down again. What had I done? And what was I expecting to happen next? Then, anxiously, I wondered if I really wanted that awkward Kevin to come here and argue with me. Well, I was in it up to my elbows now. Nothing I could do to stop the future from happening.

I had thought about staying at a local B&B for the few days I was down here — I had seen one in the village — but as the evening drew on, I felt the warmth of the old house inviting me to stay. Why not make up the bed in Aunt Jem's room and settle down there until tomorrow? I knew there was a lot to think about, and a good night's sleep would help, so I found clean sheets and some pillows in the ancient airing cupboard, and prepared myself for the night ahead.

I wondered if I would sleep — a different bed, noises in the old beams and timbers, night sounds in the woodland outside. But once I made myself a bit of supper and went up into the moonlit room, I knew all would be well. After all, so many people had lived in this house — even slept in this room, this bed — so why should I have any problems?

And I had none. Deep sleep came like a blessing, and no dreams hindered my rest. I awoke with the early light and heard birdsong outside, so got up, dressed, and made my way down to the kitchen. Shopping was going to be the most important job today, for I knew I would be staying for longer than I had planned. I smiled to myself. What had Annie Grey said? *The old house don't let you go once you'm here.* And somehow that seemed to be about right.

I was sitting on the window seat in the

living room, watching the world outside and making lists of what I needed to do, when a knock sounded on the front door. *Jake*, I thought at once, *ready to carry on with his gardening work*. I opened the door, smiling — to be faced with a stranger.

'Good morning,' she said in a smoke-thickened voice. 'I'm Meriel Fontenay, and I live in the village. I believe you're the new owner of this house?'

I nodded. Who on earth was she, this blonde-haired, middle-aged woman dressed so smartly, and with keen brown eyes that seemed to be looking around even as she spoke?

'Yes,' I said briefly. 'I own this house now that Jemima Marshall has died. She was my aunt. I'm Carla Marshall, down here for a few days. What can I do for you?'

Meriel Fontenay gave me a wide smile, and I thought I saw something in her eyes that I didn't quite like. A sort of hidden pleasure. But why?

She said — and now her voice was less harsh, her smile a bit more sincere — 'I'm delighted to meet you, Carla. And I do hope that we can do some business.'

I stiffened. 'Business? What sort of business, Ms Fontenay?'

She pulled her expensive bag a little more securely onto her shoulder. 'Antiques,' she said, and now her smile was real. 'I'm an antique dealer. I conduct my business from my house in the village. I heard you'd come down to restore this old place, so I hoped you might take advantage of my advice — and my business, if you wish to dispose of anything.'

I felt slightly shocked — everyone seemed to know I was here — and then definitely affronted. 'I don't think I shall want to sell anything,' I said firmly, 'but thank you for calling.'

She fumbled in her bag. 'My business card. Do ring me if I can be of any help. Any time; I'm usually around. Goodbye for the present, Carla.' And she turned and walked down the path.

I watched her go, slightly bewildered. I had thought I would be alone here with Aunt Jem's memories, not meeting various people who had their own hopes for the old house.

With my shopping list in my pocket, I drove into town and the supermarket. I did hope the afternoon would be free of callers. I planned to start unearthing some of my aunt's old treasures.

The morning went by with Jake appearing, having hidden his bike among concealing bushes, and then disappearing to his new allotment. *Well, at least he still wants to keep working*, I thought as I went up the creaking stairs to delve further into the few as yet unexplored rooms.

All of them needed cleaning, and I opened windows and made a list of jobs to do — working as a journalist in London had taught me to list facts and events and then think about them. Finally, only the box room — or what Annie Grey had called 'the junk room, more like' — remained to be explored.

I called Jake into the kitchen at lunchtime, offering him a bowl of (tinned) soup and a hot drink. He came willingly enough, kicking the mud off his shoes outside and then washing his earthy hands. Then he favoured me with a big grin as we sat down at the table.

'Like a sandwich?' he asked, producing a small box from his backpack. 'Beetroot and early lettuce. Try one, miss.'

I did so. It was a bit soggy, but tasty. I ate the last crumb and returned his smile. 'Thanks, Jake. And call me Carla, will you? I don't like this 'miss' business.'

He finished his soup. 'That was OK, but when I start giving you some fresh veg, you'll make real soup, won't you, miss — er — Carla?'

'I certainly will,' I told him, and got up to make coffee, wondering how on earth I had got into this weird situation. Homemade vegetable soup; a keen gardener; and someone who wanted to buy Aunt Jem's unwanted antiques. I shook my head as I offered him a mug and then pushed the sugar towards him.

When Jake went back to work, I cleared up and then returned to the box/junk room. And there, right at the back, beneath cluttered shelves and half-hidden under a curtain, I found something that warmed and excited me; a real treasure.

Aunt Jem's Memory Box.

3

It was quite a large, rather shabby box with a lid that was hard to open, though I eventually got it off. What to look at first? My eye was caught by a small parcel wrapped in brownish suede with what felt like spiky jewellery inside it, but I put it aside, eager to find what else Aunt Jem had thought worth saving in her Memory Box.

There were piles of photographs, still in their yellow packets which the developer had returned. Family celebrations; smiling faces. People I hardly remembered — perhaps uncles, distant cousins. And Aunt Jem herself in one of them, sitting on a beach, smiling and wearing a really wonderful straw hat trimmed with daisies. The last snap made me halt a minute before putting it back in the envelope — a small child, hands behind her back, looking down intently at the flowers in the border before her. A black and white photograph; no colours then.

'That's Aunt Jem,' I whispered, wondering at the dark hair tied up with a huge bow, a pretty cotton dress, and a glimpse of black, sensible shoes.

Putting aside the snaps, I then delved further and found a beautiful Honiton lace collar in need of a good wash, and some nylon stockings. Wartime wear, I guessed; highly valued and kept safely in those far-off days. But why in a Memory Box? Did they come from an American admirer? Perhaps these belonged to another relative whom I had not yet met — a cousin, or someone who had lived during the war. Not a daughter, for Aunt Jem never married, and I'd never heard of any love affairs.

When I got to the pile of torn and discoloured letters tied with a red ribbon, I'd had enough. Memories were lovely, of course, but the emotions they evoked were exhausting, even rather disturbing. So, closing the box but carrying the little suede bundle of jewellery, I went downstairs and took Jake's dusty old deck chair out of the shed, then carried it to the lawn where flowers and grass offered peace and quiet, and I thought a lot as I opened the suede parcel.

Such old-fashioned treasures. Gold-coin earrings, a pendant holding a pearl in a Tudor rose setting, and a gold bracelet big enough to decorate a bare sun-touched arm with no sleeves to hide it. And more earrings — small, neat studs of varying colours, and others that dangled and swung their precious stones against the wearer's cheeks.

I smiled as I looked at them, picking out the few that really attracted me. Then I saw a small box almost hidden in the corner of the suede covering. I opened it carefully, and then caught my breath. No old-fashioned costume jewellery here, but something I guessed was valuable, as well as elegantly beautiful. A brooch, perhaps a few centimetres wide and the same in length, bordered with tiny white stones — diamonds, perhaps? — around a silver setting of tiny clasped chains, and holding a pale green stone. I recognised it as an aquamarine, because I was interested in semi-precious stones. And then — an even more beautiful part of it — a small, elegant heart holding a pearl and outlined in those same gleaming diamonds.

I was still gazing at it, enchanted by the way sunlight enhanced its attraction, when Jake appeared. 'I forgot to tell you ... ' he began, and then stopped, looking down at the brooch in my hands. 'Wow, that's a beauty. Worth a bit, is it?'

I came out of my reverie and met his gaze. 'That's what I'm thinking,' I told him. 'Lovely, isn't it? I'll have to get someone to look at it, value it, and advise me how to keep it safe. Is there a jeweller in town?'

Jake considered for a moment. 'No; they closed last year. But Mrs Fontenay deals with this sort of stuff. You could ask her.'

I blinked. 'The antiques woman?'

'Yeah. She lives at Ferndale House, down at the bottom of the hill. She'd tell you what it's worth.'

I nodded, and started to wrap everything up with the suede covering. The last to go into the little parcel was the brooch, and I had a sudden thought. How did Aunt Jem get this wonderful piece? I said, 'It's the provenance — the history of the brooch — that I'm interested in, not just the value. Do you think she'd mind if I showed her these things and asked a few questions?'

Jake grinned. 'Why not? She looks a bit fierce, but she's OK when you get to know her. Kev did up her kitchen last year and said she was really nice.' He turned away, then back again. 'Oh, Carla — forgot to tell you. Kev's worried about me being on your land. Said he'll be around sometime soon to see you. I hope he won't turn nasty.'

My heart sank. 'So do I. Well, tell him to come as soon as he likes, and that until then it's fine for you to keep working here.'

The big grin flashed again over his shoulder as he went back towards the allotment. 'OK,' he said, and disappeared.

I sat on, my mind full of thoughts. I could probably deal with nasty Kevin, I guessed, but then I was back with the jewellery. In particular, that amazing brooch. Then on impulse I went indoors, found Meriel Fontenay's card, and before I could change my mind, dialled her number.

She answered at once. 'Jewellery? Yes, I deal in it — mostly Edwardian and Victorian. Your brooch sounds a bit of that period. Why don't you bring it round for me to see? A cup of tea, perhaps? You've got my address. I look forward to seeing you.'

She was brusque, but sounded friendly, so I decided to accept her invitation. I told Jake I was going, and would he lock the shed door if I wasn't back by the time he left? 'Put the key under the flowerpot,' I said, and he raised his eyebrows.

'The obvious place to look,' he said, but I shooed him off and went indoors to make sure I looked presentable for my first entry into village social life.

Ferndale House was an imposing villa at the bottom of the hill leading into the village, and behind it I saw several outbuildings. The front garden was formal and tidy, but it didn't really attract me with its shrubs and gravel path and not much flower colour to be seen. Which made me wonder if I might start Jake on my own garden — still time to sow seeds for the summer.

Meriel came to the front door quickly and smiled at me — a much friendlier smile, I thought, than on her visit to my old house. 'Come in. The kettle's on; we'll have a cup in the garden, shall we? This lovely sun needs to be indulged in.'

She whisked me through the hallway — heavy old bench by the door, I noticed, and some brass ornaments on the table opposite it. Of course; she was an antiques dealer. There would be old bits of furniture all over the house, I guessed. But the kitchen was modern to the extent of being almost minimalist, with shining machines and a plain marble table. A complex woman, I thought as I was taken onto a back terrace where garden furniture waited for us.

And then a man's voice came from behind us. 'Merry, where's that newspaper that's got the feature about books in it?'

She turned, smiled, and called back, 'Wherever you left it, Dan. Try the dining room.' Then she looked at me as she gestured for me to sit down. 'Men. Untidy and useless. But he's not too bad. Can't cook, of course, and lives for his books.' As we seated ourselves, she called, 'Come and meet the new owner of Thorn House. We're going to have tea out here.'

A tall, blond-haired man appeared, looked at me, then came over and held out his hand. He smiled, and I thought those sky-blue eyes were amazing. 'This is Carla Marshall,' said Meriel, already on her way back to the kitchen. 'Keep her amused, Dan, while I get the tea going.'

'Daniel Eastern,' he said in a quiet, resonant voice. 'Meriel's step-brother. I'm delighted to meet you, Miss Marshall. And even more pleased that Thorn House has a new owner. Time it came to life again. Mind if I join you?' He pulled out the chair next to me.

I was caught by his quiet manner, his blue eyes, and his general air of confidence and friendliness. I said, 'Yes, I'm pleased, too. But it's very dilapidated, and I shall have a bit of a tussle getting it looking as it should.'

Meriel came out with a laden tray. 'You'll find plenty of help in the village, Carla. All the old girls will want to come and look at you, offering help at the same time.'

Daniel stood up and began putting cups and saucers and plates around the table, while Meriel began pouring. I sat there watching and listening as they bantered with each other, and then wondered what this personable man was doing here in this quiet village, when surely he should have been working somewhere else.

He looked at me across the table and I saw his eyes, very bright and full of something that excited me. 'So you're Jemima Marshall's niece, I believe? You know that your aunt was a very accomplished author?'

I blinked. 'Well, yes, of course. We were all very proud of her when her books started to be published. I have several of them with me now, in Thorn House.'

He passed me a plate of cupcakes and said, 'The coffee ones are the best. Do try one.'

'Thank you, I will.' But I didn't eat it. Why was he asking about Aunt Jem? I wondered.

Meriel broke in slowly, without looking at me. 'Dan is a bookseller, Carla. He has a shop in town. All he ever thinks about is books, so don't let him bore you. Shall we change the subject?'

'Not yet, Merry. You can have your turn when I'm finished. Miss Marshall — '

'Carla, please.'

His smile was easy and attractive. 'Thanks. You see, Carla, from time to time in the publishing trade, something brings the past back to life. And suddenly, it seems that the children's books your aunt wrote are being bought and read again. Of course, everyone in the trade is delighted that their old books, probably hidden away in a box in a back room somewhere, are becoming almost as famous as a best-selling novel. Sales are growing.'

I took a bite from the cupcake. He was right; it was very good. But I was becoming confused. 'Well, that sounds great. But what does this have to do with me? I mean, Aunt Jem died four months ago.'

'Ah, yes,' he said, and the excitement in those attractive eyes made them even bluer, 'but you're back at Thorn House, and it's possible that you might find, somewhere in the house, the original manuscript of the missing, unpublished third book in one particular series — the one that they'll need to read to finish the ongoing story.'

We stared at each other, and Meriel filled our empty cups. 'Don't let him boss you about, Carla. I'm sure you have enough to do as it is, without searching for a manuscript.'

Slowly I was coming to terms with

what Dan had told me. Aunt Jem, a beloved author for children; and new sales of her books. And I could perhaps find, among all the junk and old things in Thorn House, the important missing story.

'Well,' I said firmly, 'I'm afraid you'll have a wait on your hands. Every room is full of what I can only call stuff. It all needs sorting out, and at the same time I'm trying to clean and restore the old house.'

Again our eyes met. Then Dan said quietly, but with a resonance in his voice that hit me hard, 'I understand all that, Carla, and I'm sorry if I'm interfering with your plans. But if you should need any help — I mean, a bundle of papers could be hidden anywhere, I suppose — I'd happily pitch in.'

Meriel cut in, with a degree of annoyance in her deep voice: 'Really, Dan, you're going over the top. Why on earth should finding this wretched story be important enough to take you out of the shop and fiddling about in Carla's house, no doubt interrupting what she's already made plans to do? Mind your manners, brother, if you please.'

His eyes met mine again, and then that smile broke out, and I knew I could forgive him anything. I started to say, smiling back at him, 'It's very good of you to want to help, and perhaps in a day or two —'

Again Meriel broke in. 'You've had your turn, Dan, and now it's mine. Carla, what about this old brooch you've found? You want me to have a look at it, don't you? Well, now's as good a time as any. Dan, take the tea things out to the kitchen, will you, and then I suggest you go back to your shop and count the mounting sales of this famous book.'

She grinned at me and I grinned back. Dan did as he was told, gathering the plates and cups and then disappearing into the kitchen.

'Well, let's see it, then,' she said; and, reaching into her pocket, she took out her magnifying glass.

4

With Aunt Jem's brooch on the tea table, we all stared at it. Dan was the first to break the intent silence. 'Whew!' he said, and Meriel raised her eyebrows.

'Yes,' she said seriously. 'Definitely 'whew'. A beautiful piece, and look how those diamonds shine in the sun.' She picked up the brooch, turned it over in her hands, and finally put the magnifier to her eye. 'Late Edwardian,' she said. 'Wonderfully set. Jewellers knew how to create such lovely things in those days. Imagine the owner wearing it, and how good it would look with equally beautiful clothes of that period.'

We all stared hard at the brooch, and she added, 'The diamonds are well cut, and the gems — especially that big aquamarine — are good types of stones. And look, Carla, did you see this?'

The back of the jewel was as elegant

as the front, and no, I hadn't seen what she was pointing out as again she turned it over. There were two rows of blue lapis lazuli stones that ran along the bottom of the silver setting. They formed two words, making me screw up my eyes as I strove to read the letters.

Dearest Jemmy.

I caught my breath. 'Jemmy?' I whispered. 'That's Aunt Jem — but how could it be?' I thought hard. 'You said it was Edwardian, didn't you — such a long time ago ... '

'Your aunt's ancestor,' said Dan, his quiet voice helping me to think more clearly. I looked across the table and met his gaze. He smiled at me. 'Was your aunt quite old when she died?'

'Eighty-one,' I said, and he nodded.

Meriel took up the tale. 'So this could have belonged to a relation of your Aunt Jem, Carla. Perhaps her mother. This was made at a time when people delighted in wearing rich jewels to balls and assemblies. Yes, this could've been a loving message to someone in your family, Carla.

But who from?' She smiled. 'We may never know — but it's beautiful enough just to admire. Or sell.' She handed the brooch back to me. 'Definitely worth a few thousand, but probably much more valuable to you as a family treasure.'

I let my fingers play over the jewel and slowly nodded my head. 'My aunt, or even her mother, who was a Jemima, too. And someone loved her enough to have this made with the wonderful message on the back. Could that have been because he didn't want everyone to see it? Someone other than her husband, perhaps?'

Silence, while we all considered this precious find. And then Dan said, quietly as usual, but with the sound of purpose clear in his musical voice, 'So Thorn House seems to be something of a treasure trove. Well, I wonder what else you might find as you search through it, Carla.' He paused, and then added even more quietly — but the words hit my mind with an impact: 'Miss Marshall's original manuscript of what could easily become her best-selling book, do you think?'

I felt doubt darkening my thoughts. Dan really was keen to find this manuscript. Was he perhaps just being charming and helpful because of what he wanted? I had thought him someone I could possibly trust, and like. A new friend, if I decided to live here, at Thorn House. But now that doubt took away my smile and made me say a bit sharply, 'I'll certainly look for it, Dan, but don't hold out too much hope. And anyway, it'll take me ages to go through each room and sort it out.'

'Of course, Carla. I don't want to rush you.' He was smiling at me as he added, 'And don't forget my offer to help if I can. I'm having a few days away from the bookshop, so I'm at a bit of a loose end.'

And so you think you can ransack my old house. I heard my voice grow cold and sharp. 'Thank you very much, but I'm sure I can manage on my own. And Annie Grey, down the road, promised to help if I needed her, so I shan't have all the work to do alone.' I got up, put the brooch back in my pocket, and smiled at Meriel, who had been listening with a doubtful expression on her face. 'Thank you so much for the tea, and for your assessment of my old brooch. When I decide what I'm going to do with it, I'll let you know. And now I really must go — so goodbye to you both. I can see myself out, thanks.'

But Meriel followed me to the front door, and as I was leaving she said, 'Don't be too hard on Dan. He's a good man, really; just caught up with his books.'

I nodded. 'Yes, I understand.' Then I walked down to the gate, turned to see her watching me at the door, and set off on my way home. Home to old Thorn House, with a treasure in my pocket.

I was glad to be alone now. So many things to think about, and so much to do. I decided that tomorrow morning I would go to Annie Grey's cottage and ask for her help — those upstairs bedrooms were all cluttered and in need of a good spring clean. Two pairs of hands would make the job easier to cope with.

As I reached the house, I thought of Jake. Would he still be here, working at what he chose to call his allotment? And what about his brother Kevin, who might, as Jake had warned, be nasty?

I took several deep breaths as I walked up the rough sloping drive that led to the front of the house, and then stopped. I had just had a cup of tea and some cake. That poor boy, digging and hoeing and weeding — didn't he need a cup as well? I went straight into the kitchen, switched on the kettle, and warmed the teapot. Then I walked up the garden and found him, just as I had thought, busily at work. He straightened up as I approached, and grinned at me, and I found it so reassuring to have someone really friendly in this haunted old garden. Not haunted by ghosts, but, as Aunt Jem had said, the presences of all the people who had lived here in the past. I had the feeling that they were all watching what I was doing, and smiling approvingly as I thought of the best way to bring the house back to life.

Jake's voice broke into these thoughts. 'Hi, Carla. Look, the lettuces are really heartening up, and I reckon I'll be picking next week. Give you one for a salad, shall I?'

'Yes, please, that would be great — freshly picked, and all your own hard work. Jake, I'm making a cup of tea, so stop your work and come and sit in the shed for a few minutes.' I turned and led the way down the garden, and he followed.

I said, 'If your brother really wants to come and see me, please ask him to make it soon. I want to get everything cleared up. I don't like the idea of him breathing down my neck. OK?' Then I nodded him into the deck chair and went off down to the house to make the tea.

Soon we were sitting in a friendly silence as I joined him in a cuppa. 'That was great,' he said when he finished. He got up, then stood looking at me, and I saw a new expression on his face. Happier. Brighter. More hopeful.

'Carla … ' He stopped as if searching

for words, and they came slowly when he found them. 'You letting me have some of your garden is really great. And I haven't forgotten what you asked. I'll be tidying up your old flowerbeds next week. It's all made such a difference — no more worrying, and all thanks to you.'

I had a lump in my throat. At least one thing was going right. I nodded at him and said, 'I'm glad to be able to help, Jake. And seeing how hard you work, I'm sure that once it all grows, you'll eventually build a small business.'

'Yeah,' he said, grinning broadly. 'Me, a businessman, eh?' And he strode off up the garden to his new allotment.

I took the empty mugs back to the kitchen and then went up to the bedroom where Aunt Jem had slept, and which was mine while I was here. Sitting down on the old cane chair, I allowed my thoughts free rein. The Memory Box; old letters and nylon stockings; jewellery and that fabulous old brooch. And then Dan telling me that two of Aunt Jem's children's books had come into the public eye after years of being forgotten, and would sell well if only the original manuscript of the third and final story could be found. So I must try and find it, to please Dan, who wanted to have it to drum up trade in his bookshop.

But did I really want to please Dan? I was uncertain. I had certainly revised my thoughts about his step-sister, realising now that Meriel was friendlier than she had seemed at first. And it would be good to have a new friend in the village, if I decided to stay on at old Thorn House.

Here my far-ranging thoughts were shattered by the sound of a car stopping on the gravelly entrance below the window, and then footsteps crunching towards the house. When a loud knock on the front door echoed like thunder, I got up, stared out of the window, and saw a shabby old Morris Minor. As I ran downstairs, instinctively I knew the visitor was Kevin Woodley, and my heart beat a little faster as I opened the door. A man stood there, looking at me with the same-coloured eyes as Jake.

'Mr Woodley,' I said, smiling and hoping to start this meeting with a friendly atmosphere.

But he just stood, and now his expression was of surprise, which slid into an answering smile. 'Well,' he said in a gentle Devon burr, 'who are you? I was expecting to see the owner of this house, not a pretty young maid like you.'

I blinked, taken aback. This was not how I had imagined nasty Kevin Woodley would greet me. 'Er — I'm Carla Marshall, and, yes, this house belongs to me.'

His smile warmed and became a copy of his young brother's grin. 'No wonder Jake's fallen for you — oh yes, he has. But then he's a strange boy, full of funny thoughts!'

We looked at each other for a stretching moment while I wondered what to say next. Then, shuffling his feet, he asked, 'Can I come in? I think we've got things to talk about.'

I backed away, opening the door a bit more. He came in at once, looking about him, staring up the doglegged staircase, and putting his hand on the wooden panelling. Then he turned and gazed back at me. 'Quite a place, eh? And you're the owner. Going to live here, are you? Or sell it, perhaps? Someone with a few million could do it up real nice.'

I blinked again. Really, I thought, what was this man doing in my house? But then I remembered Jake toiling away outside, and I said quietly, 'Why don't we go and see what your brother's doing? If he hasn't gone home already.'

Kevin Woodley nodded his head and followed me out of the house. I led him up the path and through the wicket gate, and there was his brother, picking up his spade, his hoe, and his basket of weeds and turning towards us.

'Oh,' he said, and I heard the sullen note that had been in his voice whenever he talked of Kevin. 'So you're here. I'm just going.'

Kevin grunted, and I stepped into the breach. I wanted no arguments out here. I said quickly, 'Off you go, then

Jake — everything looks good. See you tomorrow, shall I?' He nodded, pushed past his brother, and went off towards the shed; there, I knew, to clean the hoe and the spade, and then collect his bicycle, neatly hidden under some of the bushes close to the house.

Kevin and I watched him go. Then Kevin grunted again and muttered, 'Funny lad; wants to grow things when I could give him a good job. But no, he don't want to work.'

This was too much. I turned on him. 'Just take a look, Mr Woodley — look around you. All this was a rough field, just grass and weeds, and your brother is making it into a cultivated allotment — with my permission, and my approval. And you would perhaps be surprised if you knew just how hard he's working.'

He stared at me, and I saw puzzlement slide across his face. I smiled to myself. I had won a few points and now could afford to try and soften him up. 'Come back into the house and we'll talk about it, shall we? And perhaps you'd like a drink? I expect I can find something in the fridge.'

I could see how confused he was. His brother working, and here I was almost chatting him up. I watched while his thoughts become clearer, and then was smiling at me, nodding his head, and saying, 'Well, thanks Miss Marshall — I'd like that.'

We walked back into the house, where I took him into the parlour with its space and comfy sofas, and then said, 'Make yourself at home. I'll fetch the drinks.'

I went back into the kitchen and found the remains of a bottle of white wine that had accompanied my supper last night, along with some cheese biscuits, and I put them on a tray beside with two of Aunt Jem's beautiful glasses.

Excitement bubbled through me. I would charm this awkward man if I could. After all, I'd had plenty of experience working in London. But this was a new challenge, deep in the country. I smiled as I returned to the parlour.

5

'Jake tells me you're a builder,' I said, sitting down opposite where he lounged on the chesterfield, his dirty shoes on the carpet in front of him. I knew I needed to get on the right side of this man, so I raised my glass and smiled at him.

'That's right,' he said, swigging a gulp of wine and returning my smile a hundred percent. 'Got a nice little business going, I have. And that's why I want Jake to come into it. A good job that'd be — something with a future. But no.' The smile died and a tight expression slid over his lean face. 'Got to do what he wants, never mind family offering something decent.'

Before I answered, I took a good look at him. Shabby work-stained clothes, and those shoes ... But there was something about him. A keen-shaped jaw that reminded me of various movie stars, and hair that needed cutting, but was a rich brown without any sign of grey. And an air of confidence, as well as the sense that he was happy with his work and just a bit anxious about Jake. Not at all the nasty Kev I had imagined.

'Look, Kevin — you don't mind if I call you that?' Not giving him a chance to say yes or no, I went on determinedly, 'You talk about a good job for Jake, but can't you see that what he's doing could lead to exactly that? He wants to grow and then sell his vegetables — and everybody's trying to buy fresh food these days. So why shouldn't he succeed in his business, as you've obviously succeeded in yours?' *Compliments are usually what everybody wants,* I thought. Would this work? I waited.

He finished his wine, put the glass on the table by the chesterfield, and sat up a little straighter. Then he grinned at me as he said, 'Got you where he wants you, has he? Trust Jake — born a charmer, he was. But look, Miss Marshall.' Here he stopped, raised an eyebrow, and went on. 'OK to call you Carla? Nice name. But

Jake, well, he's been in trouble at school, and then he got involved in a rough gang of town boys, and I was scared he might end up in more trouble. You know what teenagers are like these days.'

I couldn't help the words that came out quickly. 'Weren't you the same, Kevin? I bet you were — until the business got into you, and then you changed and became a successful builder. Well, why shouldn't that happen to your brother?'

He just stared at me, smile gone, and a look of indecision clear on his face. 'I dunno. Maybe you're right — but well, I mean, this isn't his garden, is it? He virtually stole it. And another thing — you might suddenly want that bit of vegetable bedding to build houses on. He can't stay here; you must see that.'

I laughed, and he stared with even more doubt. 'This is my old family home, Kevin. I will never build on it, I can promise you. So just make up your mind that I'm happy for Jake to stay here and do his growing. Anything else you're worried about?'

Shaking his head, he let the grin return, but I thought his expression held something else as well. 'One thing, Carla — will you sign a bit of paper saying that Jake has your permission, just in case it all goes wrong?'

I thought for a moment. He was a businessman, after all, and knew that everything must be legal to make it workable. 'Agreed. I'll do it now. Wait a moment.' I got up, went to the bureau, found a piece of notepaper and scribbled on it, signing my name with a flourish. He might not be nasty, but he was a far-sighted man, and I respected that. 'Here you are,' I said. 'All signed and sealed. So you'll let Jake stay?'

He nodded, got up, took the paper, read it carefully, then followed me into the passage, and paused as I opened the front door. I thought his smile quite beguiling. 'Come out with me one night, Carla? I think we might get along rather well.'

I was shocked, but at the same time felt a warm glow through me. Not nasty

Kevin after all! And how nice to be invited on a date. But then the reality of what was happening hit me. I was here in Devon to clean the house and decide what to do with it, not to flirt and form new relationships. So I returned that nice smile and said as gently as I could, 'Lovely of you to ask, Kevin, but really, I'm too busy — I don't think I can manage any time off. So I'm afraid it's thanks, but no.'

An awkward silence hung between us, until he stopped smiling, nodded his head, and said briskly, 'OK, perhaps another time, then. I'll be around again. Cheers, Carla.' With that, he strode off down the rough path to his car.

I watched him drive away and then went indoors again. But not for long. Kevin and his admiration of the house, his concern for his brother, and his invitation stayed in my mind, and I couldn't get rid of them — until I remembered I was going to call on Annie Grey and ask her to come and help me tomorrow. Quickly I put all thoughts except the present moment from me, and went down to find Rose Cottage.

Annie's door was open, and I smelled a tantalising aroma coming from the small thatched cottage, which had roses all around the garden fence, as well as every sort of flower you could pick out of a garden catalogue. Such a beautiful sight. I paused on the doorstep, wondering if Jake could possibly get my own neglected garden to grow like this. And then Annie was beside me, grinning and looking at me, and then back at her garden.

'Bit untidy,' she said, 'but that's how I like it. Everything coming up at once. Well, Carla, how's that boy of yours getting on? The village thinks you might have trouble with his brother — a big fellow with a nasty temper, they say.'

I wanted to laugh but managed not to. Village gossip was something I remembered well from my teenage years at Thorn House: *Going out with boys, she is — what's her auntie thinking of, then?* And when I had brought Alan down to meet Aunt Jem, it was even worse.

Heard how he's a fortune-hunter from London? Knows Miss Jem has money. Poor Carla — hope as she doesn't get too involved with him. How Aunt Jem and I had laughed when these wicked tales reached us.

And then I had left the village — with Alan — and forgotten all about them. But now I remembered, and realised that the life of our little community hadn't changed at all: keen interest in everybody, especially newcomers to the village. And so I must expect to be singled out and gossiped about, until they all knew what I intended to do with Thorn House.

Then I remembered Kevin's invitation, and was thankful that no one had been around to hear what he said; see how he looked at me, and my way of turning him down. What a glorious story that would make! So I must keep myself to myself — at least until I had decided what the future held for me.

I smiled back at Annie and stroked the opening petals of a delicate pink lupin, recalling a drift of them growing in the

garden at home. My smile died. Home
… was I thinking of Thorn House as my
new home?

Quickly, I turned to Annie. 'You said
you'd help me with those cluttered bedrooms? I'd be so grateful. Could you
come tomorrow morning?'

At once she said, 'Why yes, of course
I'll come. So much to do there — cleaning and dusting, Carla — and I guess that
between us we'll find some old treasures.
Your aunt was one for hoarding, you
know. Bertha told me that …' Which left
me wondering what else garrulous old
Bertha had told her.

★　★　★

The next morning Annie and I looked
at Aunt Jem's bedroom, mine for the
moment, and already showing signs of
a new and untidier occupant: shoes by
the wardrobe, bed unmade, and a T-shirt
dropped carelessly on the floor by the
window seat.

Annie, uncoiling the vacuum cleaner,

looked at me with a laugh lifting her lined face. 'Not so tidy as yer old auntie, are you, maid? A place for everything and everything in its place, she used to say.'

I smiled back at her, but my thoughts were suddenly full of Aunt Jem. I knew she hadn't married but had loved children. Had she longed for them? How blessed I was that her love had been lavished on me after Mother died.

I got out of Annie's noisy way and tried to remember what we were doing. Oh yes, cleaning up. So I dusted the dressing table, opened drawers, and then realised that I must recycle everything I could; in particular, the clothing. And if Aunt Jem had been a bit old-fashioned in her choices, at least all her clothes were of quality and looked elegant. Someone might be glad to have them.

Thoughts of the missing manuscript made me look for secret drawers, but nothing appeared. Then, after shaking the dusty curtains and promising them a blow on the clothes line when I had managed to put one up, I looked at the beams in the ceiling, saw cobwebs, and directed Annie's vacuum at them. No spiders on my bed, please.

The noise ceased and Annie said, 'That's all done, then. Time for coffee, maid. Shall I bring one up? And then there's that little box room to do. Full of junk, I saw as we passed it.'

We chatted as we sat companionably on the window seat with our mugs of coffee, and I looked out over stretching fields and stands of woodland that finally became part of the far landscape. Dartmoor, with its tors and valleys and slopes of wild growth, was a magical, mysterious part of Devon.

Again my childhood memories grew vivid — all those picnics; those walks with Aunt Jem telling me the history of the nearby village or ancient dwelling we had just passed. And once again I thought, *I can't possibly go away from all this.* The warmth and the welcome of the old house caught me, and my emotions surged.

Finishing my coffee, I pushed away

such thoughts and got up. I really must try to be positive. 'Right then,' I said to Annie, 'it's time to go and see what that awful little box room holds.'

It was chock-a-block with things Aunt Jem — or Bertha? — had thrown away: not taken down to the dustbin or a recycling centre, but just put in the box room, no doubt thinking, *I'll see to them later.* I could just imagine Aunt Jem's voice as she consigned all the rubbish to somewhere out of sight.

Well, we had a real job on our hands. First of all, we had to force a way in. A dressmaker's dummy — Aunt Jem had dearly loved to sew — stood just inside the door, frightening the life out of Annie. 'Oh my!' she cried. 'Thought it was one of them ghosties.'

I stared at her. 'What ghosts, Annie? In this house? Do tell me.'

She recovered herself, pushing aside the dummy and trying to get further into the little room. 'Oh, don't worry yourself, Carla. No one's seen anything, but that old Bertha said she heard footsteps and felt cold when she thought someone was creaking down the landing.' Our eyes met and she grinned reassuringly. 'But yer auntie told her off. 'No ghosties in here,' says she, 'only memories of happy people who loved living here. Stop imagining things, Bertha, and get on with your work.' But for all we knew, Miss Jem imagined things herself. All those book she wrote … ' She found her way to the bleary window and opened it wide. 'Whew, thank goodness fer fresh air.'

I worked with her for the next half hour, and by the end of that time the box room had a new look to it. There was still work left to do, but we had cleared out a lot of old rubbish, which stood on the landing behind us, waiting to go downstairs and be thrown away or recycled. We had so far found nothing of any real value. A fur coat — but whoever would want that now? And a few rather battered old hats, along with shoes and an occasional evening dress. 'Pretty, that,' said Annie. 'Have it made to fit you, maid, and you'll look ready for the next party.'

I laughed but said I didn't think that was a good idea.

All the time, my mind was focused on the missing manuscript. I looked under the camp bed, behind all the remaining bits of furniture, even under the faded rug that lay on the dusty floor. No papers. And so at last we shut the door on the box room, put away our dusters and the vacuum cleaner, and went downstairs, telling ourselves that we'd done some good work.

Annie had brought down, among all the other rubbish, a decidedly shabby dressing gown. 'Look,' she said, pointing at the label. 'Jaeger — that's wool, isn't it? I'll get it cleaned, and then it's just the job fer when we have another cold winter. Do you mind if I take it, Carla?'

'Of course not, Annie. I'm glad that it's still usable. Looked in the pockets, have you? Might find something valuable there — a five-pound note, perhaps?'

We laughed as she put her hand into one pocket and said, 'Your old auntie was very absent-minded, you know. Let's see what's there.' She drew her hand out, looking disappointed. 'Nothing. But better look in the other one … '

I watched, already thinking of other things: Jake, the brooch, Daniel Eastern, even Kevin Woodley. Until Annie held a bundle of scrappy old papers under my nose, saying, 'Better than nothing, I suppose. Here, Carla, here's some reading for when you're sitting in the garden this afternoon. And now I'm going home — same time tomorrow?'

I said yes, and heard my voice as if from the distance — because as I looked at this bundle of papers, I knew exactly what she had found. Aunt Jem's unpublished manuscript of the third book in her stories. Here, in my hands.

6

Standing there, unaware of anything other than the papers, I looked at them and held my breath. This was what Daniel wanted; what a publisher would pay a lot of money for so that they could put it in print and then happily allow the public to buy it. What on earth would Aunt Jem have thought of that?

Slowly I sank into a chair, still staring at the papers. Did she ever imagine that her final story in the three-book series would eventually come to light? Had she forgotten it? Or had she not even wanted it published? My thoughts whirled and delved, but I came up with no answer, until I realised that to find out a bit more I must read the story. And yet I felt I shouldn't do so. Was it possible that Aunt Jem, with her fine imagination, had foreseen me finding the manuscript? So perhaps she did want me to read it.

Confusion raged inside me.

But at last my mind stopped its chaotic wonderings, and I put the papers into my leather briefcase which stood beside the dresser, waiting for me to take it somewhere more sensible. After all, when I went back to London and my job as a journalist, I needed to know exactly where it was, filled with notebooks and pens and my small tape recorder. Also the maps of London, so that I knew how to get to whatever venue was on the day's list. The papers were safe there, and I would read them later on in the afternoon, when I would sit out in the sun and give myself time to read — and then think.

For lunch I made what Jake called 'proper soup'. He had given me the first turnips, and I had a basket of onions and some potatoes and a few carrots, plus a few chicken legs in the freezer which would make good, tasty stock. And then I realised I needed an activity to stop my mind racing. I worked until Jake appeared at the door, his grin reminding me that, papers or no, life went on, and I was involved with things other than Aunt Jem's stories.

Jake hovered in the doorway, and I saw him looking at the cooker with its steaming pot of soup on it. 'Smells good,' he said. 'Is it those turnips?'

I felt myself quieten down as I smiled at him over my shoulder. 'Amongst other bits and pieces,' I said. 'Sit down and I'll dish it out.'

'Great,' he said, going to the sink and washing his hands before coming back to the table and a chair.

And yes, the soup was tasty. I looked at him and said thoughtfully, 'Just shows you what good you're doing, Jake. I bet lots of people will buy your vegetables. How's everything growing up there?'

He cut another slice of bread, and offered it to me before taking one himself and then looking at me. 'Rain, I want some rain. I'll have to water if this dry weather goes on. Must get a watering can from somewhere.' A pause, and I saw him thinking. 'I'll ask Kev. He's got all sorts of things in his old shed. Bet there's a watering can.'

A pause hung between us, and I broke it, saying gently and not looking at him, 'Your brother feeling better about you being here, is he?'

I wasn't prepared for his answer, which was so quiet that I thought he was talking to himself. 'Yeah. Better 'cause he's met you. He likes you. Wants to take you out, doesn't he? He said so last night.'

His eyes questioned me across the table, and all I could do was force a smile, finish my soup and say brightly, 'He did ask me. I'm just so busy.'

We said no more, but Jake had another helping of soup and then said he must get back to work. I nodded and watched him take his soup bowl to the sink and leave it there before heading for the door. He didn't say any more, and I wondered anxiously if I had added to the family squabbles. But I knew that going out with Kevin Woodley wasn't at all what I wanted to do.

I sat in the old deck chair and put Aunt

Jem's manuscript on my lap. Something was telling me I needed courage to read her unpublished story. Well, I reckoned myself as being a brave twenty-first-century woman, so what was I waiting for? I removed the unmarked first paper and started to read.

The story was about children. The main character, Katherine, was a child who had been adopted but was not aware of it, and was finding it hard to keep up her lifelong friendship with the neighbour's family. 'So where've you come from? That old house up the lane? You don't belong here.' Jimmy was eight years old, and delighted in tormenting everyone and everything — flies, butterflies, the family cat, and the girl from the old house. He wanted new friends, not the dull old ones.

His sister, little smiling Debbie, was quite different — even disposed to keep up the friendship that had lasted all Katherine's life, living in the Devon countryside with Aunt Hannah. In the story she frowned at her rude brother and said, 'You can come into our tent if you like, Katherine — we're going to have a picnic in there. Mother has made a treacle tart, oh, goodie!' Katherine, of course, had said yes please.

I read on. There were small episodes, building up the relationship between aunt and the adopted daughter, but never revealing the truth. Shopping in town, buying new books, new school uniform, having eyes tested — all the things that made up Katherine's life. And there were adventures, of course, Katherine taking the leading part in most of them: saving Debbie when she slipped into the stream running through the garden, watching the goldfish, taking Jimmy to his mother when he cut his finger, trying to make bows and arrows; even saving the cat stuck in the apple tree, carrying the ladder and risking wild scratches as she brought the scared animal down again. Such adventures, and such a gripping story for a child.

I read half the pages and then stopped, lifting my head and staring into the distance. I watched Jake, who had started weeding the wild border. He bent down, pulling a strong weed that was trying to suffocate a tall plant with big leaves and huge green flowers. Then something jumped inside me. That plant was angelica — a strong natural healer, Aunt Jem had told me. She had picked the stems, making the bits crisp and crunchy and decorating cakes with them. Yes, angelica, and here was the story girl doing exactly that.

The picnic was taking place: Katherine had taken slices of Aunt Hannah's cake with her for the meal. 'These green bits are lovely, so crunchy and nice. Do you want a bit of mine, Jimmy? You've finished yours.'

He scowled. 'Don't like eating flowers.' He puffed out his cheeks and grinned at her. 'You'll probably die now, greedy guts.'

The papers rustled on my lap as a breeze touched them, and I tided them, reading on as the story continued with a big adventure about Katherine saving

Jimmy from some terrible disaster, and winning praise from her aunt and Jimmy's parents, and even Jimmy smiling at her as he murmured, 'Thanks, Katherine.' But I hadn't reached the end yet, and I felt suspicions growing in my mind as I read on.

At the penultimate page I stopped, sensing that the end of the story would surprise me. I had recognised myself on Aunt Jem's pages — all those events and small thrills were what had really happened, part of my life at Thorn House. The story ended with Katherine picking a small posy of the white blossoms of the May tree and giving it to Aunt Hannah as she went in one evening.

'Not supposed to be lucky, Katherine — but we'll change the old story and make it lucky, shall we, love?' And then later, Katherine had heard the old servant who loved to gossip asking Aunt Hannah an unexpected question. 'Does the maid know that she was adopted, Miss Hannah? Quite a thing for a young child to accept, I reckon.'

On the last page, with feelings of love and alarm mixing inside me, I read Aunt Hannah's reply. 'No, she has no idea. Remember that I adopted her when her poor mother died without having children, and we have grown very close since then.'

Again, I left the last page and tried to accept what I had just read. Finally I made myself read the last scene, where Aunt Hannah said, 'One day I'll tell her that I longed so much for a child that I decided to adopt her. You see, I chose this motherless baby and made her my own, and she has been mine ever since that long-ago day.'

In the story Katherine ran into the kitchen and hugged her aunt, happy to be loved, and knowing that now she was one up on the kids on the road. 'I was chosen — they were just born,' she told herself as the story came to an end.

After what seemed a long time of thinking and feeling, I was Carla again, sitting in the sun, watching Jake pile all the rubbish in the wheelbarrow and disappearing. My thoughts were a jumble of surprise, alarm, and finally love as I accepted slowly that although Aunt Jem's story had ended happily, for me it had brought the beginning of a new story.

7

It took me a long time to settle my disturbed thoughts. So in the story, Aunt Hannah's child was adopted, and memories told me that she wasn't writing about a fictional Katherine, but a living Carla.

During that evening I tried to get my mind clear and to accept the message in that book. I was an adopted child, and not the niece of the aunt who had taken me in when my mother died in childbirth, which was what I had been told and accepted. It was rather a shock, and one that had my mind racing as I thought back, remembering how Aunt Jem had treated me like her own. I realised how wonderfully lucky I was that such a sweet, loving and generous woman had chosen me and given me the life I now enjoyed so much. I couldn't blame her for not telling me; no, I would rather go on thinking I was her child. It would be difficult, but as the evening ended and I went up to bed, I knew that I had made a wise decision, and one I would not change.

I stood by the window, watching the moonlight shifting over the trees and shrubs, Jake's vegetables, and the mysterious thorn tree climbing up the wall towards me, and knew then that Thorn House was my home, whether I remained here or not. Home — such a warm, comfortable word, and I was saying it silently to myself as I got into bed and closed my eyes.

★ ★ ★

But the next morning my thoughts were far from settled and easy, for I knew I must decide what to do about the manuscript of the third book. Dan Eastern wanted it, but should I give it to him? Publication of Aunt Jem's final story would reveal a lot about me, both to unknown readers and also to all my friends and colleagues. I imagined a column in the local paper about Aunt Jem's heiress finding it and releasing it for publication. There would be pictures, even quotes, if they could get me to give them. And I would hate all that.

It was, of course, the same thing that I did in my job in London, interviewing people and then writing up all that they had said, what they meant, and perhaps — particularly — what they would have rather kept quiet about. I had loved that life … until now. Now I understood what the person who had given themselves away must feel like. So no, Dan would not have the manuscript.

When Annie Grey tapped at the door and greeted me with a big grin, I suddenly made a decision. 'Today it's the parlour, please, Annie. I'm having friends to supper tomorrow, so a good turn-out is just what's needed. And while you're doing that, I must find decent glasses, and perhaps give the silver a rub-over. I want the parlour to look its best when I lay the table.'

I phoned Meriel at once. Answering, she said she wasn't at home but at an auction in town. She was brisk, ending our brief conversation quickly. But her message was clear — she would love to come to supper tomorrow, but Dan must speak for himself. 'He's in the shop all day; here's his number ... '

As I went about getting things together for the proposed meal and then wrote a list of ingredients, I thought about ringing Dan, but then decided instead to call in on him. After all, I would be in town shopping, so it would be easy to stop by his shop.

In this I was mistaken, however. As I headed for the bookshop, I felt stupidly nervous — how ridiculous! From what I had felt about him at our earlier meeting, I thought he was a kind man who would easily decide to accept my decision to keep the manuscript of the final book to myself. But if he didn't? And then I remembered his air of determination, and the steely look that could temper his blue eyes into icebergs, and I frowned. But surely it would work out? I would look around his shelves, perhaps buy a book, and chat about everyday things — the fine weather; my neglected garden responding to Jake's hard work — and we would end with both of us smiling and saying, 'See you tomorrow, then.'

But it didn't happen like that. When he saw me, he at once came to the door and looked at me with expectancy on his lean face. 'Good to see you, Carla — have you found it?'

I blinked, surprised at this sharp question. So he wasn't quite the charmer I had thought. But I gave him a big smile and allowed him to draw me into the little shop. 'What a greeting, Dan!' I said lightly, and at once he returned my smile, looking slightly ashamed.

'Sorry about that,' he said in a placating voice, and gestured me towards a couple of chairs beside a coffee table laden with the day's newspapers. 'Do sit down. Like some coffee? I'll put the machine on.'

I sat, looking around me. There were shelves crammed with books, some very soft music playing in the background, comfortable chairs, and what should have been a warm welcome. I heard voices in the back room into which Dan had disappeared. 'Thanks, Lily, you do it better than me.'

He appeared again, smiling. 'My colleague knows all about coffee machines. Now, Carla, tell me what you're doing in town. I've been imagining you busy with dusters and window-cleaning gear. How's the old house looking after the spring clean?'

This was the moment. Should I tell him or not? I started going on about the dusty bedrooms and the box room full of junk, and then stopped as a young woman came in with a tray of coffee. So this was the gorgeous Lily, with highlighted hair and the slimmest waist imaginable. I watched as she smiled sideways at Dan, who responded with a brief nod, though I thought the look in his eyes said a lot. She poured the coffee, put a plate of biscuits in front of me, smiled again, and retreated behind the counter at the front of the shop.

For some obscure reason, I felt deflated. Then I started imagining things — was she Dan's girlfriend? But if she was, why should I care? I knew I did, though, and sudden anger rushed through me. *All right, Dan Eastern, you can have the beautiful woman if you want, but you shan't have dear old Aunt Jem's last story.*

Somehow I drank the coffee, even ate a biscuit, and went on about Jake and the way he was bringing the old garden back to life and how good his vegetable plot was looking. Then I asked the question I had brought with me. 'Dan, I've asked Meriel to come to supper tomorrow night — and I wondered if you'd like to come, too?'

At once the blue eyes lightened and the charming, hard-to-resist smile surfaced. 'Great! Thanks, Carla, I should love to come. I imagine Meriel said yes?'

I got to my feet. 'She did. And I'll expect you both around seven — you might like to look at the garden before we eat.'

'That would be very interesting — and I'd like to know a bit more about the ancient thorn tree decorating your wall.'

Heading for the door, I saw Lily smiling at him, but this time there was no response on his part. Instead he came out into the street with me and said, 'Delighted to see you, Carla. And I hope you'll come again and next time look at the books.'

We both laughed a bit at that, and I said, 'Perhaps you shouldn't spoil your customers with such excellent coffee — I was too busy drinking it to think about books.'

Our eyes met, and I suddenly knew what he was thinking. *Has she found the manuscript or not?* But I was in no mood to talk about it. Let it all wait until the right moment came, when I could carefully tell him about finding it, and explain my decision, which I hoped he would accept.

I walked up the street to the car park, and drove home, my thoughts still disturbed. Was it Lily, or the worry about how Dan would react to my decision, that was unsettling my mind?

Annie greeted with one of her sly, amused looks. 'Telephone message,' she said.

'Who was it, Annie?'

'Dunno. Didn't give his name. Sounded cross you weren't here.' Amusement faded to keen interest, and I guessed she expected an answer that would feed her gossipy mind.

'Thank you.' I wasn't giving an unnecessary answer, and so turned away into the kitchen to unload the shopping. But I guessed who the mystery caller must be — Kevin Woodley, of course. Putting the bread into the bin, I shut the lid with a bang. I didn't want Kevin Woodley ringing me, because I knew he wanted to ask me out. I would of course turn him down again, but I feared that his obstinacy and determination meant that this call was one of many more to come.

Between us, Annie and I restored the old parlour to its remembered comfortable beauty. It was a big room with dark wood-panelled walls and oak beams holding up its ancient ceiling. As a child, I had loved sitting here by a blazing log fire, watching Aunt Jem perhaps scribbling in a notebook, or just sitting near me and smiling while we discussed the day's events.

Now, as Annie collected her bag and cardigan ready to leave, I took a last look around the room. 'Thanks, Annie, you've done a good job here.'

She nodded, grinned and said, as she headed for the door, 'I'll be here same time tomorrow. Another bedroom to do, and then there's the attic — if I can get up there.'

A vision of her stuck halfway up a ladder brought my immediate answer. 'I think we'll leave that for the present,' I said hurriedly. 'There's enough junk still filling the box room, and I can't cope with any more yet.'

After she had left, I admired the parlour. The room looked wonderful and inviting. It was now dust-free, its huge old windows clean and shining, and the big oak table had been polished to a gleaming patina. I told myself that flowers were all that was needed to enhance its old, familiar elegance.

Out I went, and found Jake weeding the top of the border, a huge pile of leaves and dead flower heads littering the lawn, waiting for the wheelbarrow to take them up to the new compost heap he was making at the bottom of the garden, next to the hedge boundary and overlooking the field next door. He stood up straight as I approached, and stretched his back and arms.

'Hot work,' he said, grinning, and I smiled back.

'Take a break, Jake. There's some lemonade in the kitchen — help yourself.'

'Well … ' He was doubtful, but I told him not to be silly; after a rest, he'd be ready for another hour's work.

I was alone in the garden, and a strange feeling spread through me. I had had fantasy-style adventures here as I was growing up. There were magic trees, and the song of the stream bubbling along beyond the hedge, carrying a message, I had imagined. Jimmy and Debbie and

I had built a camp under the big rhododendron bush. I smiled, remembering; and then a question came out of the blue. Where would I be, and what sort of life would I be living, if Aunt Jem had chosen another small child to become her own? And again, that feeling of gratitude and sense of being in the right place filled me.

I picked white narcissus, blooming half-hidden where I recalled them being, and then a huge scarlet blossom from the rhododendron bush. A few wildflowers caught my eye in Jake's allotment — primroses, one or two cowslips, some lime-green euphorbia, and one beautiful purple hellebore, creating a small but lovely bunch with which to decorate the parlour table.

I went back toward the house, knowing I needed a background for these beauties; and then, standing by the thorn tree, I decided to pick a few sprays. Its vibrant leaves surrounding small white buds, a few of them in full flower, were inviting and pleased me enormously. Never mind the old superstitions — today the white

May blossom would come indoors and delight both me and my guests. I smelled its strong, exhilarating fragrance, though was also quickly reminded that there were thorns where you least expected them. With a scratched finger, I went back into the house to add the final touch to the gleaming parlour.

8

My guests arrived in good time, Meriel saying she had enjoyed the short walk from her house in the valley, and Dan parking his open-topped car on the rough pathway leading to the house. I greeted them warmly, glad to have made new friends.

'It's a beautiful evening — and doesn't this hawthorn smell amazing?' Meriel stood in front of the thorn tree and bent to sniff the small white flowers, and at once a memory hit me.

'We used to eat the leaves and call them bread and cheese when we were children,' I said. 'That was village folklore. Can't remember what they tasted like, though.'

Dan stood in the open doorway, glancing into the kitchen as he said, laughing, 'I bet they weren't a patch on whatever you've got cooking in here, Carla.'

Meriel said dryly, 'The way to a man's

heart — we know the rest, don't we?' She followed me indoors. 'But it smells wonderful.' And then she stopped and stood in the parlour doorway, catching her breath. 'What a room! Look at those panels. This house must be really old. And it's all yours. Carla.' Swinging around, she smiled at me. 'What a lucky woman you are. Niece of a famous author, and now finding a new home out of the rat race. You're not going back to London, surely?'

I frowned uneasily. 'I don't know yet. After all, my work is there, you see.'

Meriel raised a thin eyebrow. 'Why not bring your work here? There are lots of home-based businesses these days. I know I couldn't bear to leave here if I were in your shoes.'

Dan was looking at me with what I guessed was curiosity. I thought that all this about me living here in Thorn House had only one interest for him: would I find — and give him — the third story of Aunt Jem's famous trilogy?

I knew the time had come to stop talking about me and get on with our friendly meal. So I found a beaming smile and said, 'I haven't made up my mind about anything yet. Now — can I offer you a drink?' Looking at Dan, I guessed how his mind was working — *If she leaves, I'll never get my hands on that vital manuscript.*

But he waited while Meriel said a sherry would be nice, and then he said quietly, and with a smile that warmed my uncertain heart, 'Let's think about something else, shall we? Like just what it is in your kitchen that smells so good?'

At once, my anxiety was gone. I laughed, saying, 'It's duck in orange sauce — and I only hope that neither of you are vegetarians?'

Dan joined my laughter. 'I'm definitely a meat-eater — and Meriel has bouts when she eats only vegetables, but I bet she'll tuck into this marvellous-smelling duck tonight! And yes, please, I'll have a glass of whatever wine you have.'

We ate the meal, and it was very good. As I dished out creamed turnips, I said, 'These are Jake's first offerings of home-grown vegetables. He's also got beans growing and the first lettuce ready to pick.' I caught Dan's eye across the table. 'You said you'd be interested in seeing the garden. Shall we go out after coffee?'

He nodded and gave me a charming, warm smile that made me smile back and think how lucky I was to have found new friends here — especially Dan, who I sensed had interests that were similar to my own.

Later that evening, we wandered slowly around the garden, ending up at Jake's allotment. Meriel wandered ahead of Dan and me, looking at the runner-bean tripod Jake had built. To my dismay, Dan turned to me and asked, 'So, what news of your aunt's manuscript, Carla? Have you found it yet?'

I couldn't reply for a moment, my thoughts panicked. Should I tell him that I had indeed found it, but wasn't prepared to give it to him? I stared at him intently while trying to resolve my indecision. I saw his blue eyes grow dark and piercing, and then I made up my mind.

'Yes, Dan,' I said steadily. 'I have found it, and the story provides a good ending to the first two books. But ... ' I took a deep breath. 'You can't have it. I'm keeping it. Sorry, but ... well, that's how it has to be.'

The blue eyes were cold, and that attractive smile faded to a tight expression of determination and disapproval. 'I see,' he said. 'And is there nothing I can do — or say — to make you change your mind?'

I forced myself to stay calm. 'Nothing. It's staying here, with me. Sorry, Dan.'

Meriel returned to my side, praising Jake's hard work, and then caught Dan's eye. She said smoothly, 'It's been a really lovely evening, Carla, but it's time to leave this wonderful old place, I think. Thanks so much for everything.' Her smile was warm. 'Hope to see you again soon. Yes, my turn to entertain next, isn't it? I'll look at my diary and then give you a ring.' She turned towards Dan. 'Come on, then. You with your car, and me traipsing down the lane.'

Dan was smiling again. 'Give you a lift, if you like.'

She laughed and put her arm through mine, and together we walked back towards the house. 'No, thanks,' she replied to Dan's offer. 'I shall enjoy looking at the hedges and hearing the birds getting ready to roost.'

Outside the open door, we stood and gave the thorn tree a last sniff. Then Meriel was off, with Dan following behind her, and I was alone.

I went back into the kitchen and started piling up dishes and saucepans, but my mind was busy with what had just happened. I had made a final decision, and probably put an end to the new friendship that I had felt was starting with Dan. It had begun so well, and now it was over because of my obstinate feelings about Aunt Jem's manuscript. But as I cleared the kitchen and then thought about going to bed, I found my mind was no longer doubtful, and I knew I had done the right thing, whether Dan liked it or not.

After all, he had never shown that he was attracted to me. So why was I worrying?

'But at least I have a good friend in Meriel,' I told myself, and that felt hopeful and reassuring.

I was restless in bed, and even thought I heard noises outside, but then decided it was a sort of dream. When I awoke the next day, I looked at the clock and saw I had slept for nearly seven hours. A new day, and who knew what might happen next?

★   ★   ★

What happened was a shock, and a nasty one. I was waiting for Annie to appear when Jake came to the door. 'Carla ... ' he said, and I saw at once how agitated he was.

'What is it, Jake?' I took his arm and drew him into the house. His eyes were wide, his pleasant young face overridden with what I took to be anger. 'Tell me,' I said quickly, and pushed him onto a chair.

He drew in a big breath and looked at me. 'I thought they were my friends.' His voice rose, the words pouring out. 'Thugs, more like. They've taken all my veg, pulled down the bean tripod, and walked over the seedlings. There's nothing left that they haven't trodden on or pulled up. Friends, huh!'

I put a teabag in a mug and switched on the kettle. 'Here, drink this. So who were these so-called friends who did this? And why would they have done?'

'Boys I knew at school and went about with. Bad company, Kev said. But they were fun.'

I nodded. 'They were at a loose end, I suppose. Not working? Just messing about?'

He nodded, stared down at the table and muttered, 'And I was just as bad. But not now. I'm working now; I've got a future planned out ... but they've gone and spoiled it all.'

The kettle boiled, and I spooned sugar into the steaming mug. 'Drink this; you'll feel better. And don't look so upset. It's not as if your allotment has been taken from you — you'll just have to start over again.'

I smiled determinedly at him, and he gave me a faint grin as he drank his tea. 'Yeah. Do it all again. Yeah, I can do that. But, well, I don't know what else to say.'

I watched him as he sipped his tea and began to look a bit more hopeful. 'It's not the end of the world, Jake,' I said, smiling and trying raise his spirits.

'I suppose not.' His voice was back to normal, and he tried to smile back at me. 'But it's rotten, isn't it, your friends playing a dirty trick like this.'

'Life's not all fun and laughter, Jake. These nasty things do happen, you know. But why should those boys have done this, I wonder?'

He pushed the empty mug across the table and got to his feet. He seemed an inch taller, his chest broader, and the expression in his eyes told me he had recovered from this unpleasant prank. He would rebuild his vegetable beds, I knew, and he had learned a useful lesson about life as well.

'I saw them a couple of nights ago, and they laughed at me when I said what I was doing. But I told them to — to clear off. I said I wasn't keen to go out with them now. So I suppose this is sort of revenge, isn't it?'

I nodded. 'And revenge is a dirty deed, and a dirty word. Try and forget, Jake. Now, would you like me to go out there with you and help get the beds back in order?'

He stood by the open door, looking back over his shoulder. 'No, thanks. But you've been great, Carla. The tea was good. I don't know what I would've done without you.'

'Oh, you would've managed. Off you go, then, and I'll have coffee ready later in the morning.'

When Annie arrived soon afterward, she asked, 'What's that young man doing out there, with all that mess around him?' She came in, taking off her cardigan and putting it on the chair with her bag. Her eyes were sharp, and I knew I must explain to satisfy her curiosity. So I told her all about the night's bad work.

'Oh my, those naughty boys — never know what they'll do next. Have to get digging again, won't he?' She shrugged and shook her head. 'Now, I'll be in that box room, sorting out all that old stuff.' And she was gone, collecting a bucket of cleaning gear before stomping up the stairs.

Thinking about Jake, I went outside and looked at the thorn tree, almost in full flower now. The scent was strong and made me think of wild gardens and wild people, perhaps with old secrets.

'I bet you've seen a few odd things,' I muttered. 'If you could only tell me some of your stories.' Smiling at such stupid thoughts, I went back into the kitchen, trying to think clearly.

Should the police be told about this raid? I pulled a face, almost hearing the voice of a police officer saying, 'Just a minor crime, madam. Unless you have any evidence — is there any CTV on your property?'

Of course there wasn't, not here in the middle of the countryside. Forget the police, then. But I knew I should tell someone. And then it came — Kevin, of course. Jake's brother. He must definitely be told.

When Jake appeared for mid-morning coffee, I asked him for his brother's phone number. He looked alarmed. 'Not going to tell him, are you, Carla? He'll say it was all my fault.' But with Annie agreeing with me that Kevin must be told, at last Jake reluctantly gave me the mobile number. 'He'll be at work. He may not answer.' I could see that he hoped his brother would ignore the call.

However, when I rang, he answered at once. 'Kevin Woodley.'

'Carla Marshall,' I said, and there was a short silence. Then his voice changed; the crisp business tone was gone, and he sounded polite and friendly.

'Good to hear from you, Carla. I hope you've decided we might have an evening together, have you?'

'I'm afraid not,' I said shortly. 'I'm

ringing to tell you that a horrid prank was played on Jake last night.'

'Is he all right? Is the boy OK?'

'Yes, nothing to worry about. Except that some of his friends have ruined his allotment. They must've come in the night.'

'Ah, no, that lot jump a car and joyride around. Didn't you hear anything?'

'I did, but I thought I was dreaming.'

'I know that bunch of kids, the ones Jake used to go around with. I'll sort them out. See their parents.'

I felt a glow of relief. Things were seeming to work out. I said, 'Thank you, Kevin. Jake knows I'm phoning you. He's up there now, trying to get the allotment sorted out. He — he's a good boy, you know.'

'I know that. But he's been a real worry till now. Sorry, Carla, I've got to go — bloke wants to talk to me about the job I'm on.' No goodbye, just the call ending and me still holding the phone.

I sat still before going up to the box room and seeing what Annie had done in the way of cleaning. I thought Kevin Woodley had sounded worried about Jake and the damage done to his allotment. Halfway up the stairs, I decided that perhaps brother Kevin wasn't quite the obstacle in his life that Jake thought him to be.

9

It was late in the afternoon when I decided to fill a quiet hour by finding the bundle of letters still lying in Aunt Jem's Memory Box, and read them. I was halfway up the stairs, heading for the box room, when I heard the unmistakable sound of a vehicle parking in the drive. Not quite the smooth purr of Dan's expensive car, but something I vaguely recognised.

At the bedroom window I looked down and saw Kevin's shabby white van, emblazoned with a big black sign reading KEVIN WOODLEY, BUILDER. Alive with wonder, and a little uneasy, I went downstairs, muttering, 'OK, Kevin Woodley, Builder, and what are you doing here when you should still be at work?' On the bottom step, I added, 'No good pressing me for a date — haven't you realised that yet?'

I opened the kitchen door and stood there waiting, but for what I had no idea. Then Kevin marched past me carrying a spade and a garden fork, and only just glancing at me as he went on up the garden, saying, 'Hi, Carla.'

'Oh — er, hi, Kevin …'

And then I understood why he was here — to help his brother remake his spoiled allotment. The thought was heart-warming. I must do something to help too, I told myself, and at once went in and switched on the kettle. Tea and whatever was in the cake tin would surely be welcome to those hard-working chaps up there, and also indicate to Kevin that I was glad to see his show of support for Jake.

I would leave reading those mysterious letters upstairs for later on — perhaps this evening, when I would be alone again.

Hard work was the name of the game up there in the allotment, both men digging and bending down, Kevin swearing slightly when an obstinate weed eluded his spade, and Jake looking at me as I arrived carrying a tray. 'Time for a break,' I said cheerily. 'Sugar, Kevin? And I know about you and three spoonfuls, Jake.'

They straightened up, looked at each other, and then almost sheepishly came towards my tray of goodies. I opened the cake tin and sliced huge wedges of lemon drizzle cake. 'Help yourselves,' I said, putting the tray on the ground and then sitting beside it. A nettle stung my leg, and a bee buzzed around my face, but it didn't matter. What did matter was the expression on Kevin's face as he folded himself down beside me, and then pushed the tin over to his brother.

'Have a go at this,' he said, and I saw an unexpected twinkle in his eye. Then he looked at me and smiled. 'Good of you to bother, Carla. And I reckon we're about ready for a breather. Hard work, this.'

It was pleasant, I found, sitting there munching cake and listening to Jake and his brother making plans. Jake still sounded a bit sullen, however, when Kevin asked him what he thought he should do. 'What am I going to do —? Well, what d'you think? Start the whole thing over again. Yeah, I know you've helped with the digging, but now I'm going to have to go and buy some plants — I can't let my source of vegetables get behind, can I? Not if I want to sell them. Which I do.'

I waited, wondering just how things would work out, until Kevin said, 'OK, that's what your plan is. So let's leave all this and get to the garden centre. No time like the present. We'll buy your plants and drop them off here, and then you can put them in tomorrow morning. Sound good?'

Jake finished his tea, got up and looked at the disturbed long bed with its straggling, half-dead occupants. 'Yeah,' he said, and I heard a change in the tone of his voice. He looked back at his brother. 'Thanks, Kev,' he mumbled. 'Yeah, that's what I want to do.'

I got up, collected our empty cups, and put the lid on the cake tin. 'It's time for you to go, anyway. So you'll drop off your plants, and then I'll see you tomorrow as usual?'

'Yeah,' said Jake. 'Thanks for the tea, Carla. I'll put the tools away and then get my bike.'

Kevin picked up his spade and headed for the garden shed. 'Maybe it'll come in handy.' He slapped Jake's shoulder, and his voice was full of amusement. 'When your business gets off and you employ half a dozen staff, eh?'

'Yeah.' Jake actually smiled.

Kevin opened the shed door. 'Go and put your bike in the back of the van — you'll need that tomorrow. And get a move on — shop'll close soon.'

I waited outside the kitchen as finally the white van drove off, but not before both Kevin and Jake had grinned and waved goodbye to me. Then I went into the house, wondering at what life was doing these days, and I thought, *Well, this afternoon has been a lesson; Kevin's turned out to be a good guy, and Jake realises it. Can't grumble about that, can I? And now I'm going to look at those letters.*

They were there in the Memory Box,

the red ribbon half-untied and the first bit of paper crumpled. As I looked at them, I felt an uneasy stab. How private were they, written by someone I didn't know to someone else? Was I right to want to read them and delve into the past? But I knew I felt strongly about them, for surely they would tell me a little more about Aunt Jem's quiet life. Then I wondered — if they were important enough to keep, what could they have said to her? Remembering what I had learned about my adoption, I decided that they must have contained something that was vital enough to keep. A secret, perhaps?

The first letter was written in the late seventies, and the address was somewhere in Kent, where I knew Aunt Jem had lived before the woman I had thought was my mother wrote these letters. And it was addressed to *Dearest Jem*. Something caught at my breath, but I read on. The dark blue ink had dampened and some of the words were difficult to decipher. But I got the meaning.

You know that I lost the baby, my lovely

daughter, the one I had such hopes of. And Dr Eames has told me I must have no more. So now I realise I shall remain childless for the rest of my life. I feel so sad, Jem — can you imagine? But then, of course you can. You, too, longed for children, didn't you, even when we were still at school. And then your Peter died; and later, when Jack Leonard left you, I saw your face when you understood that all your hopes for the future were finished.

I dropped the page of the letter and thought very hard. All this was adding up to a sort of story built by my mother and Aunt Jem. A story in which the newly found third book of her series brought about a happy ending. My mother (but not my mother) dying with the second baby — how right Dr Eames had been to warn her about another birth. And Aunt Jem, hoping so much and for so long to become the family auntie loving her nieces and nephews, took what she thought was the only sensible way ahead. And so I was adopted.

For quite a time I sat there on the window seat in my room — Aunt Jem's room — thinking about this sad story. Sad for the woman I had thought to be my mother, dying in childbirth, with no son or daughter in her life — for clearly her husband had either died or left her; and she was alone.

The last letter but one in the small pile was from Dr Eames himself, informing Aunt Jem that her only sister had died along with the newborn baby. He expressed sympathy in a polite way, and I wondered how she had managed her life after that letter had arrived.

And then, in the final letter in the small bundle, written in a strong hand which was black and ominous, was the last turn of fate in Aunt Jem's life. It was a love letter from Jack Leonard, and I knew at once that he was the final love in Aunt Jem's life — but he had left her, and then had written this last letter from the United States of America.

Dear Jemmie, sorry not to have written before. Things have been difficult here.

My job is more demanding, and Amy has decided to take me back after all, so I won't be coming to England to claim you as we'd both hoped. You know I loved you, but now I have to do all I can for Amy, who is going to have a child. I do hope you understand. I sent you some nylons not long ago, but here is a little farewell gift, full of my love, and just a bit more precious than stockings. It's a family heirloom, a brooch sent by someone to the woman he loved. I send you the same message as the brooch carries. I still love you, Jemmie, but it can't be. Your Jack.

It took some time for me to understand this sad little story of two women who longed for children but never had any, and I wondered at their bravery in just going on. But what could one do in life? We all had to 'go on'. Which took me back to the present day and my own life.

Before putting the letters back in the Memory Box, I took out the brooch and wondered what I should do with it. I closed the box and then decided, as I went downstairs, that from now on I would live my life to the full. And how blessed I was to have been adopted by dear Aunt Jem. I just hoped I had somehow given her pleasure in raising me from a small child. And then her words came back to me, warm and seemingly fulfilled: *'Carla, love, I always thought of you as my own.'*

Downstairs, the house awaited me. It was big, warm, and full of what Aunt Jem had called 'presences' — dreams of the people who had once lived here. Pouring myself a glass of wine as I cooked a bit of supper, I thought of all the problems and disasters that had probably befallen these forgotten people.

A little later, after I had eaten and was longing to get out into the garden, a new thought came to me, which helped to shift the grief of reading the letters. Those old people had loved, too, as well as living through difficult times. And I knew intuitively that amongst those secret lives, love had been one of the most important gifts.

I stood by the thorn tree before I went indoors again. The moon shone in the eastern sky in a silver arc, and the flowers smelt of history, and new hope for the future. It was just what I needed. I went up to my bedroom and had a dreamless night.

*　*　*

The next morning I was cheerful and full of new ideas. When Aunt Jem had been left alone, she had gone on. And that was exactly what I planned to do — go on. I would start by explaining to Dan Eastern why I had initially said that I didn't want the manuscript to be published. I at least owed him that — and maybe he would have some advice for me. For now I was in two minds about my decision. Surely I also owed it to Aunt Jem and her adoring readers to share her final story with the world?

After going up to the allotment to make sure Jake was there, I smiled as he proudly showed me the plants he and Kevin had bought last night. 'They'll grow well, and be ready about as soon as the ones those thugs spoiled, I reckon.'

His grin was infectious, and I was still smiling as I returned to the house and got ready to drive into town and talk to Dan. I was a bit wary of letting him know the secret part of Aunt Jem's story, but I knew I had to tell someone. And I had a feeling he would understand.

10

Annie's voice stopped me in my tracks when I picked up my bag and car keys the next morning. She was obviously up in the allotment, and I heard her saying, 'That's all right, boy. You need a few new plants after they bad boys messed it all up — and I got some to spare, so that's all right. Look after 'em proper, and they'll grow good.'

When she appeared, she was grinning; and as soon as she saw me the grin grew even bigger, making her lined old face a picture of pleasure. 'Gave that boy Jake some of me runner-bean plants, I did. Well, I heard about they bad chaps who finished 'em off for him, and I felt sorry and wanted to do something for the lad.' She came into the kitchen, saw me with my bag and swinging the keys, and said at once, 'You going somewhere, then?'

'Going into town.' I smiled. 'You heard

about the allotment being spoiled? Who told you?'

She stared at me as if I were an idiot. 'Why, the whole village knows. Gossip gets around here easy. I expect all the men are keeping an eye on their plants, in case they bad lads come again.'

'Oh,' I said, surprised and a little shocked, 'good of you to give Jake some of your plants, Annie. I'm sure he appreciates it. Now, about the box room — do you think you could finish it off this morning? I'll be back before lunch and see you then.'

'Right ho. And take young Jake a drink, shall I, like you do? Elevenses?'

I nodded. So what with Kevin helping last night, and Annie producing plants, I thought Jake must be feeling a bit better today. However, I went out to the car thinking that if village gossip worked this quickly, what would they all say if Aunt Jem's final story was published? And then that brought me back to Dan. What would be his reaction to what I was planning to tell him?

The town was busy, and I walked slowly towards the bookshop, figuring out what exactly I would say. Going in through the open doorway, I still hadn't really decided. Dan saw me and came across the shop, holding out his right hand and taking mine. Then he gave me one of those irresistible smiles that lightened his eyes and added brightness to the day.

'Great to see you, Carla. Come on in — I'll get the coffee going.'

I sat down in a comfortable chair beside the table and said the only thing that came into my bemused mind. 'Have you got the hang of the machine now? If so, I'd like a nice strong cup, please.'

He laughed and disappeared from view, and I thought what a stupid thing it was to say, as if I'd come here simply to drink his coffee. Then I saw the woman working by the shelves at the side of the room, the beautiful Lily.

She looked back at me and smiled. 'I think he knows how to work it. But men are so useless in kitchens, aren't they?'

I nodded, returned the smile, and waited until Dan came back with a tray. He poured two cups and then sat down, looking at me intently. 'So what's this all about, Carla?'

His quiet, confident tone reassured me. I thought of him as a friend, and my mind cleared at once, the words rushing out without any more thought. 'Dan, I need your advice. As you know, I've found Aunt Jem's manuscript — but it's all about me.' I heard my voice catch as emotion swamped me. 'It's personal, private stuff, which is why I said I didn't want it published. You see, I don't know what to do — and I thought you might be able to help.'

He looked across the table and nodded. 'I'll do whatever I can,' he said quietly. 'Of course I will. But I need to know a bit more. I mean, about the personal things you say it contains.'

I sipped my coffee. Stupid thoughts distanced me from what I ought to be saying. 'This is good stuff. Glad you've mastered the machine.'

His expression told me that he was a sensitive man, aware of my disturbed mind and willing to help if he could. But then a customer came into the shop, saw him, and said demandingly, 'Can I have a word, Mr Eastern? Our book club ... ' she began, and then carried on in a flurry of words that I didn't bother to listen to. I was trying to sort out the muddle in my mind.

When the woman left, favouring Dan with a tight smile, I was still worried and uneasy about what to confide in him. He didn't sit down, but stood beside me, smiling apologetically and lifting an ironic eyebrow as he said, 'I thought book clubs were peaceful gathering places, but I'm changing my mind.' He paused and sighed. 'Carla, this isn't the place for un-interrupted talk — why don't we go and have a meal somewhere tonight, and you can tell me everything that's bothering you?'

Everything? I thought. Was that the answer to my problem? But the idea of being alone with Dan and discovering more about him — for I felt he would be a sympathetic listener — brought a smile to my face.

'Yes, I'd love that. Thank you. And perhaps you're right — later on I'll tell you ...'

Then another customer came into the shop, and quickly he turned away from me, saying rapidly as he did so, 'Great. I'll pick you up about seven. OK?'

I nodded and left. My heart felt easier and my anxiety had lessened. I was sure Dan would listen and then advise me what to do for the best. My best, his best, Aunt Jem's best.

I drove home, savouring the sunshine on the trees and hedges, and found Annie in the kitchen talking to someone. It was Meriel, and she gave me a smile, holding out something long that was wrapped in gift paper. 'A little present for Jake,' she said. 'Have I your permission to go into the garden, Carla?'

'Yes, of course. Let's go together, shall we?'

We went out into the sunshine, and I

119

felt very glad that I had this new friend. A small voice inside my head whispered that I might tell her my secret, but not at this moment. Clearly the gift for Jake was more important.

We found him at the end of the long vegetable bed, bending down and putting small green plants in the earth in neat rows. He looked up and straightened his back, giving us both that wide grin. 'Annie gave me these broad beans. They'll soon grow in this weather. Good to eat, Carla.'

We smiled and made complimentary comments on his hard work. Then Meriel said, 'Too bad that you were invaded and your beds rucked up — so-called friends, were they? But look, I've brought you a very necessary present.' She handed over the gift and Jake took it, staring as he unwrapped the paper. It had a worn dark wood handle, and at the end were two small frightening things that looked like the tines of a small fork. For a moment he said nothing; then he looked at Meriel and said hesitantly, 'Well thank you, Mrs

Fontenay, but — what is it, exactly? I never seen one of these before.'

She laughed. 'A dysher. An old tool specially made to dig up dandelions.'

We stared at it. 'Well,' said Jake, with a smile on his face, 'thanks very much. It'll come in handy all the time — I never seen so many of those things as I have this year.' He moved a few steps away, onto the grass, then bent and applied the dysher to a large yellow dandelion, which came out clean in his hands, root trailing beneath it. He grinned again. 'It works! Thanks very much. Very kind of you, Mrs Fontenay.'

'I was so upset to hear about your allotment being raided, Jake, and just wanted to tell you that you're doing a wonderful job. And I hope the dysher helps.'

'Yeah, it will. Thanks again.' He bent down started work once more, putting the small plants into their neat, orderly row.

I looked at Meriel. We smiled at each other, and carried on walking down the garden. 'How's the clearing up going, Carla?' she asked.

We paused beside the thorn tree. 'It's

getting done,' I said. 'But … ' I paused. I couldn't tell her about my problem, could I?

To my surprise, she put her hand on my arm and said, 'I expect it's all posed a few difficult thoughts — getting rid of things always does. But I'm there if you want to unload anything that's worrying you. And I'm sure Dan would say the same — he's a brisk businessman, I know, but his heart is warm and he feels for people.' She looked me straight in the eye. 'Just don't let him make you do what you feel you shouldn't.'

I caught my breath. After a moment's silence, I said, 'How do you know I have problems, Meriel?'

She chuckled. 'I have one of those busy minds, picking up people's reactions and knowing what's going on in their heads. A few centuries ago I would've been labelled the village witch!' The chuckle became a full-throated laugh, but her gaze was warm and I nodded gratefully.

'Well, if you think like a witch, you can tell me some of the old tales about this beautiful May tree. Doesn't it look gorgeous now it's in full flower?'

Meriel nodded. 'Indeed it does. And one thing to remember, Carla — don't let young Jake try and prune it. I'm sure he loves cutting overgrown things down, but not this one. You see, I have a feeling that it holds your luck, and is planning your future.'

I had no words, simply a feeling of something released in my tight bundle of emotions. Of course she was only joking, but suddenly I thought of the generations of people who had lived here before and revered this old tree. Could she possibly be right? I knew then, as we walked down the path to the lane, that this was something I must think about very carefully.

Indoors once again, I watched Annie pack away her cleaning gear and said goodbye to her. Then I thought about the evening, and about Dan coming to pick me up. Ridiculously, the biggest issue in my mind was what I should wear. Smart trousers, or that new maxi-skirt? I went upstairs to try and decide.

Dan drove up just before seven, and I was ready, suddenly feeling delighted to see him. 'Come in,' I said. 'A drink before we go, perhaps?'

'No thanks,' he said, his gaze enveloping me, and I thought at once, *I hope he likes the skirt and new top.*

After locking the door, I got into the car. As he sat down beside me, Dan gave me one of his amazing smiles and said quietly, 'I like the blue ensemble, Carla. But then you always look lovely, no matter what you wear.'

I caught my breath. I didn't know what to say, so I kept silent, but a great surge of warmth — and was it excitement? — swept through me.

We drove out of the town, and then through leafy winding lanes up to the foothills that gave way to Dartmoor. I took in the lowering sun glinting on granite tors, and small groups of ponies foraging on grass and wild plants; and as I did so, the heaviness that had plagued me since reading Aunt Jem's manuscript began to lift.

When Dan pulled into the car park of a small thatch-roofed pub, my mind had cleared, and I knew I was ready to tell him my secret. But not until we had eaten a very good meal of locally reared beef and village-grown vegetables, washed down with a light, dry wine, did the opportunity come.

He sat back in his chair, looking at me with clear blue eyes. His expression was gentle, and I was aware yet again of how attractive he was. Leaning across the table, he reached for my hands, which were folded in front of me, and held them in his own. He said in a low yet vibrant voice that reassured me, 'So tell me what's on your mind, Carla.'

I met his gaze, moving my hands within his gentle grasp, enjoying their warmth and strength, and found it easy to tell him. 'I've just found out that I was adopted, Dan. I've learned that Aunt Jem wasn't my real aunt. She took me in when my so-called mother died in childbirth, and ... ' My voice was unsteady. 'And I don't know where I came from, except an adoption institute. It's frightening, because, you see, I'm not sure now who I actually am.'

11

I lowered my head because I didn't want him to see the tears that threatened to fall. His hands around mine tightened and made me look up at him. His voice as he spoke was quiet, and so gentle that I was able to blink away the tears, looking up and meeting his gaze.

'I'll tell you who you are. You're Carla Marshall, a lovely woman down from London to restore your late aunt's old house. You are going to do a wonderful job of making Thorn House hospitable and welcoming, just like your aunt did. You're making new friends, you have an excellent gardener, and very soon you're going to accept that you were an adopted child. You see … ' His eyes smiled at me, reassuring and warm, as he added, almost whispering, 'You are loved. You know you are. So why this worry about adoption? Does it matter so much?'

I sighed, a deep breath that filled my chest and somehow made the problems of my life seem suddenly to lighten. 'Yes,' I answered. 'But it was a shock to find out that I don't know where I come from, and even the legacy of Aunt Jem's wonderful love can't stop me from wondering.'

A silence hung between us, until I said, mastering the emotion swamping me, 'What you said sounds lovely, Dan — but I'm not sure it's enough. You see ... ' And then I stopped. My memories were so real that I had forgotten I was sitting here telling Dan about my life. He was almost a stranger, after all; someone whom I had only recently met. So why should I tell him about the brooch, the letters, the nylons, and the disturbing facts I had read in Aunt Jem's third story?

I decided that my secrets would remain mine a little longer, for I recalled with a quick flash of anger that Dan was only interested in getting hold of the manuscript and publishing it. Success and more income, that was what he wanted.

Not a load of miserable memories and fear of the future.

Now I knew what to do. Pushing back my chair, I got up, slung my bag over my shoulder, and headed for the entrance to the pub. I didn't say anything, didn't look back, just kept on walking — until I came to his car, and then I realised I must stop. We were in the middle of Dartmoor, and very soon night would cover everything. I had no real idea where we were, and no transport of my own. And so I waited, my confused mind full of thoughts that varied from dismissal of Dan to the idea of telling him everything and enjoying his offered friendship.

Now darkness hid the pub from view. I heard a dog barking somewhere in the village, felt suddenly cold, and wished I had brought some sort of jacket with me. Then I heard footsteps approaching. They stopped, and I realised Dan was close to me, his hands searching for mine, his voice holding that gentle resonance I so enjoyed.

'Let me help, Carla. Don't be so sad.

I'm sure between us we can sort things out. Let's get away from here; Dartmoor is frightening at night, so dark and remote. Let's drive — then come back to my flat and we'll talk. Come with me, will you, love?'

I stared at his shadowy face. He had called me *love* — and immediately something new and safe spread through me. I released my hands from his and said, 'Yes, let's do that.'

At once he walked me around to the passenger door, saw me into the seat, and then bent over me. 'A good meal, wasn't it? And I'm so handy with the coffee machine now; I'll make some at home and we can be comfortable together. Easier for you to talk, perhaps.' Then he closed the door and came round to the driver's seat, and we drove slowly down the dark lanes with their overhanging branches until we found ourselves in the town again. And eventually in his flat.

It was an upstairs apartment, situated in a handsome Georgian house on the outskirts of town. There was a small, neat

130

garden, and some chestnut trees enclosing it, making it almost invisible from the street. We went upstairs in silence, but as soon as Dan unlocked the door and I entered the flat, I caught my breath.

'How lovely this is,' I said. So ... elegant.'

'Glad you like it. Sit down and I'll get us some coffee.' He went out of the room and I sat down in a comfortable chair, which helped me to relax, and looked around. There was a fireplace filled with a big jug of green leaves, their colouring echoing the shades of the wallpaper and cushions on the two chairs standing invitingly not far away. Thoughts crowded into me. This was no typical bachelor's home; I knew instinctively that a woman's hand had been busy here. Dan wasn't married — but had he a partner who lived here with him? Beautiful Lily from the bookshop, perhaps? I should have asked Meriel about her step-brother before accepting a date with him, I thought wryly.

And then Dan was back, and we sat

opposite each other, sipping coffee and looking at one another. 'Comfortable?' he asked.

I nodded and smiled. 'Very. Your home is beautiful, Dan. Have you been here long?'

His own smile diminished, and he looked down at his half-empty coffee cup. 'I've been alone here since Janine moved out, and that's a year and a half ago.' Again his eyes met mine, and I knew somehow that he and Janine had been happy. But now he was alone. Sympathy bubbled up in me, and I wished I could say something that would tell him how I felt for him. But no words came, and foolishly I filled the moment by drinking my coffee.

And then, from nowhere it seemed, the right words were on my lips. 'I'm sorry, Dan. You must be very lonely — like me, at times. I mean, life is so strange, the way it lands a problem in one's lap.'

He was smiling at me again — a hesitant lifting of those straight lips — and there was a warm shine in his blue eyes.

'Yes,' he said. 'And that's the moment when we need friends. And loved ones. You see, Carla, whatever happens, you have to go on — though ideally with help, if it's there to be had.'

I felt very close to him in that moment. 'Yes,' I said. 'And you've done that? Of course you have. And you're advising me to do the same?'

He nodded. 'And if I can help, then I will. So — are you ready for that second cup?' His voice was steady again, and I knew this was the moment I had been waiting for all evening.

'No more coffee, thanks. But I want to tell you about me, and Aunt Jem, and the problem I'm so confused about.' Leaning forward, I looked into those sky-blue eyes and saw they were warm and smiling. And then I knew what I was doing, and I felt so grateful to Dan for helping me to sort out my muddle.

'Well,' I began, 'I found the manuscript — Aunt Jem's third book — in the pocket of an old dressing gown while Annie and I were clearing out the box room. When

I read it, I'm afraid I was rather shocked.' I stopped, and saw him settling more comfortably into his chair.

'And?' he prompted, and at once I started telling him everything.

'You see, that final book that she wrote was all about me, as a child. A child playing with friends in the village, and finding it hard to understand why they sometimes mocked me. And then there was a passage in the book where Aunt Jem and her maid were talking about me being adopted, and I overheard, and at once felt lonely because I had no real relatives at all, as I had foolishly believed Aunt Jem to be. Now I understand about the children thinking me odd and different.' I stopped, remembering, and it all came back, vivid and troubling.

It was all there in my mind — the remainder of the book, the adventures comprising a believable plot for children to enjoy reading, and then Aunt Jem telling the troubled little heroine that she lovingly thought of her 'as if you were my own'. And then the happy ending where the little girl understood that though other children were born into their families, she was special, as she had been chosen.

I stopped abruptly. Well, that was the story Dan had been waiting for, so what did he think about it? We looked at each other over the space between us, and suddenly he got up, came across to my chair, and pulled up another one close to me. He sat down and looked deep into my eyes.

'First,' he said quietly, 'I must thank you for telling me all this. It makes it quite plain how you feel about being adopted, and why you think this book, if it's published, would make life difficult for you, your friends, and your family. I understand all that, Carla. But please let me try and help you get over these lonely, lost feelings.'

His hands reached for mine, enclosed them, warmed me, and made me feel that at least here was someone who sympathised with my foolish emotions. I blinked away the threatening tears and gave him the best smile I could find — watery, weak, but a smile nevertheless. He responded at once.

'Look,' he said in a brisker voice, his smile broader than mine. 'Let's forget about the book. It hardly matters.'

'Oh, but it does,' I cut in quickly. 'It's your chance of publishing something that was lost but now is found, and which would perhaps make you a heap of money. We can't just forget that, Dan.'

He stroked my hands. 'Money can't possibly compare with your happiness. And that's all I want, Carla. Believe me. You can forget about your adoption, and make a new life knowing that even if your Aunt Jem wasn't your true mother, at lease she cherished you as her own.'

We gazed at each other, and I felt the release of all the troubled emotions that had so disturbed me. He was right — I had been loved; right from the first years when the adoption society gave me to Aunt Jem. I thought about her feelings; how anxious she must have been. What sort of child was I? How would I grow up?

And then I had an instinctive knowledge that all the strength she needed during my life with her had been a true burden of love. If I had loved her in return — and I knew that I had — then what was I doing allowing myself to feel so foolish and sad? My life had been blessed, and now I knew I must forget the past and focus on the life that lay ahead.

I took my hands away from Dan's and smiled at him — a real smile, warm and strong — as I said gratefully, 'You're right, of course you are. Lots of children are adopted, grow to love their new parents, and try to help them when they get frail and old. Which is what I did, so perhaps I can relish those last moments with dear Aunt Jem, allow her book to be published, and then get on with my life.' I stopped, and then asked, 'Do you think so, Dan?'

He got to his feet, stretching out and carefully pulling me up with him. He looked into my eyes, and I saw that the vivid blue was understanding and warm. 'Yes, Carla,' he said quietly, with his arms around me, and an easy smile lifting his straight lips. 'I do think so, and you know that you can count on me as a friend — and I'm sure Meriel would want to be included in that.' His voice had deepened, and I felt a forgotten sensation of longing fill me. He went on, slowly, quietly, and yet every word sinking deep inside me, 'And so, for now, I think we need to make a contract between us — not about the book, but about us. Because I think I'm falling in love with you, which is something I thought I'd never experience again.'

'A contract of love?' My voice was unsteady, but my feelings were strong.

He drew me closer, bent his head, and kissed me. In that magical moment all my sadness disappeared, and in its place was something wonderful.

12

Dan drove me home, back to Thorn House, and walked up to the door with me, pushing aside the thorny branches of the old tree as we passed it. I didn't know what to say, for all I could think of was that we had kissed, and now we had a contract of love. But words came, because I never wanted this night to end.

'Would you like to come in? A nightcap, perhaps?'

His arms enclosed me as he said in his low, vibrant voice, 'No, thanks. You see, I think we both need a quiet night — such a lot to think about. So ... '

We drew together, and gently he kissed me again. 'Goodnight, my love. See you tomorrow, perhaps.' Then he walked back to his car, leaving me alone in the open doorway, but with my thoughts full of happy memories.

Yes, we would meet again very soon.

And then — what? As I went up through the dark house to my bedroom and got undressed, I began to think more seriously. Dan and I had experienced what we both liked to say was the beginning of love, but how right were we? After all, wasn't a kiss after an enjoyable meal, where we had talked openly to each other, just the natural ending to a pleasant shared evening?

I got into bed, switched off the light, and then found I couldn't sleep. My thoughts roamed. Now that Dan was alone, was he also wondering how seriously I had taken his romantic words about a contract of love? Or was he instead pondering how he could persuade me to give him Aunt Jem's third book? After all, he was a businessman — and a book addict, as Meriel had warned me. Perhaps even a man with an obsession. I wasn't sure of anything that had happened this evening. And then, mercifully, I drifted off to sleep.

★　★　★

Jake appeared in the kitchen doorway the next morning. He grinned and held out a roughly folded bit of paper. 'From Kev,' he said. 'He came to see you last night, but you were out. And he came back looking like thunder!' The grin gave way to barely concealed laughter. 'Anyway, this is for you. And now I'm back to the veg. You have an awful lot of slugs here, Carla.'

'I know. It's because of the stone walls, where they live. Sorry about that!' I returned his smile, and as I went back into the kitchen I opened the bit of paper and read Kev's few words. Clearly hurriedly scribbled, I had trouble deciphering them, but a second reading revealed the message.

'Carla, glad rags on as I'm coming about seven to pick you up. Don't say no again, it's time we got together. Love, Kev.'

Love? Whatever was he thinking? I made toast and coffee trying to clear my mind. Last night's delight was still glowing, but then the thought of spending time with Kevin Woodley was a growing shade of uneasiness and definite irritation.

Somehow the hours passed. Meriel rang, inviting me to supper on Saturday night. 'Dan says he'll try to come,' she said acidly. 'But if he doesn't manage to forget his wretched books for a few hours, I'm sure you and I will find enough to talk about. Oh, and I have a bit of interesting information about your brooch.'

We laughed, and I felt that a pleasing warmth was growing in this new relationship. Yes, Meriel and I would be happy enough chatting and enjoying the supper.

As I ended the call, Annie came in to tell me that she'd finished in the box room. 'At last,' she said, ''tis clean now.' So we made plans to spring-clean the china-laden dresser filling one kitchen wall. She grinned at me as she put her hat on, ready to leave. 'How's that old thorn tree bin treating you? Any surprises? And what about May Day celebrations? Flowers comin' out nicely, jest about ready for the special day.'

I stared. 'I don't know what you're talking about, Annie — and no surprises.'

But as the words left my lips, I knew that wasn't true. What about Dan and our contract of love? Then, as I said goodbye to Annie, I remembered that Kevin and I had a date, which was another surprise — and not such a happy one.

I went into the garden and looked at the budding thorn tree. My thoughts circled, and almost without knowing what I was doing, I put out a hand and stroked one of the strong green leaves, hearing myself whisper, 'So you need a celebration, do you? Yes, I like the idea of that. We'll have a party; and you, May, will be the most important and beautiful guest.' Then, shaking my head at such nonsense, I went back into the house, telling myself, 'Yes, we shall definitely have one.'

★ ★ ★

I spent the afternoon fiddling about in the newly cleaned rooms. In the airing cupboard I found folded throws and cushion covers, and it pleased me to use them wherever I thought suitable,

143

adding a bit more colour to each room. Then I had a cup of tea in the garden as I watched Jake weed a bit more of the neglected border, and thought about the coming evening. First — and how ridiculous to worry about it — what should I wear? Glad rags, he'd said. And then I thought I could have got Kev's phone number from Jake and rung to give him a believable excuse not to go. Because I didn't want to. And it was only when Jake came to say goodbye, telling me, 'Kev's had his hair cut. Said he must look smart for your date,' that I realised it was too late to say no thanks. With another big grin and a wicked chuckle, he was off. 'Cheers, Carla, see you in the morning.' And he cycled off down the lane, leaving me with more confused thoughts about the coming date.

A haircut, and perhaps the dirty jeans would be changed for something a bit cleaner. Then I realised he was going to a lot of trouble, which was something I grudgingly appreciated. I pictured the scene, him driving up in his old van and taking me somewhere to eat and drink. Then I wondered a step further. Surely he already had a girlfriend, so why come chasing after me?

And yet the idea stayed in my mind: a man who badly wanted to get to know me better, and someone with whom I could perhaps find pleasure, spending a brief hour or two together. So I went and looked in my wardrobe. There were the skirt and lovely top I had worn for Dan. What should it be for Kevin? I grinned to myself. *Kevin, or even Kev.* Not a name I particularly liked, but a new thought came to me. Perhaps he wouldn't have the same autocratic manner that Dan had. Perhaps he wouldn't want to take something from me that I didn't want to lose. Perhaps I might end up enjoying his company.

Five minutes to seven and I was in the kitchen, waiting for him to arrive. I knew I would hear the rattling van as soon as he drove it up the track. I took a last look in the small mirror on the wall and thought I was dressed very suitably.

Sharp, well-cut grey trousers, a slightly paler grey silk shirt, and a shocking pink patterned scarf round my neck. Not bad. I was dressed for a drink in a pub, which was where I expected to be taken, not for a highly sophisticated dinner somewhere out on the moor.

And here he was, a strong rap on the door and a pair of bright hazel eyes looking at me with obvious admiration. 'Wow!' he said, smiling widely. 'You look like a girl in a fashion magazine. Hope I'm smart enough to be seen with you?'

Something critical faded from my mind as I looked at him. The haircut was good, the trousers clean and summertime-white, and the dark blue shirt showed off his muscled arms and his strong neck. *He looks quite handsome,* I decided.

I went to his side. 'Well,' I said, raising an eyebrow, 'this time lucky, Mr Woodley. So where are you taking me?'

His laugh was easy. 'A good little hideaway where you wouldn't normally go — and where they'll stare at you looking like that. Ready, then? Let's go.'

He reached and took my hand, and together we left the house and went down the path to the track where I imagined the white van would stand. But no, here was an almost new sports car with an open roof.

'Goodness, Kevin.' I was lost for more words.

His grin was memorable, and suddenly I realised this was a big moment for him. Kevin the builder, dressed to kill, and in an elegant almost-new car, with a smart young woman at his side. I returned the grin, feeling a burst of warmth for him. *Well,* I thought, settling myself onto the smooth leather seat, *what fun this is. I'm going to enjoy myself — with Kev.*

He drove around the lanes a bit too fast for my liking, but then, on the main road into town, we really roared along and I realised what a good driver he was. On the outskirts of town, we turned down a small road and stopped outside what looked like a private house. Then I read the notice — Freddie's Bistro — and at once felt a prick of excitement.

Kev led me up the path and we entered through a small doorway, to be greeted by a guy who looked like a prize fighter. His voice boomed, and his small eyes lit when he looked me up and down. 'Hi, Kev,' he said, grinning. 'So who's this lovely lady? And whose car is that outside?'

Kevin seemed to take no notice of all this cheeriness, and simply said, 'Hi, Freddie. Got a table for two? And I hope you're cooking your usual chicken in a pot?'

'I am,' said Freddie. 'Straight from France. Just got two dishes left. Here, this table do you?' He pulled out a chair and bowed theatrically to me. 'Here, lady, park yourself here. And you, mate, can sit opposite. All comfortable? Right — so what'll you have to drink?'

To my surprise, Kev looked across at me and asked, 'Wine, Carla? What sort?'

'Dry white, please,' I answered, and smiled at him. This was turning out to be a new sort of evening — this scruffy little cafe/restaurant in a small house, and this gigantic chef returning to his kitchen.

Kev and I exchanged amused glances, and then, when the dishes appeared, ate them with great relish. Small though the place was, it had a certain ambience, and instantly I wondered what Dan would think of it. My smiled faded, and Kev was looking at me with a concerned expression.

'Something wrong, Carla? Food not OK? Don't like it here?'

'No, Kev, nothing's wrong. It's all — well, very good. But you see, I have a few private problems that suddenly pop up and stop my enjoyment. Foolish, I know, but it's hard to switch off.'

His hand reached across the table and covered mine. 'Cheer up, love,' he said. 'Problems are made to be resolved, you know. Like Jake and me, getting on better now. Problem all over. So what's wrong in your life? Like to tell me? A problem shared is one forgotten. Come on, Carla, spill the beans.'

For a moment I just stared at him, too confused to speak. But then it all came pouring out, my voice so low that he frowned and leaned over the table to hear me. 'I found out that I'm adopted — just the other day. And — and, you see, Kev, it's really upset me.'

His fingers were strong, hard and warm. And his voice, when he replied, was gentle and very un-Kevin-like.

13

'A lovely girl like you shouldn't worry about a little thing like that. Traced your adoptive family, have you? I bet they were glad to see you.'

I slid my fingers out of his grasp and frowned. He didn't understand. I took a deep breath and, without looking at him, said unsteadily, 'Yes, I have. You see, I was brought up in the old house thinking my Aunt Jem was my biological aunt. But she'd actually adopted me, and I didn't know that until a few days ago I when I found some letters.' I couldn't go on. I had told Dan all this and he had been wonderfully reassuring. But Kevin was staring at me amazement, and I knew at once I should never have told him.

His voice was less loud than usual, and he was frowning as he said, 'But even if it has upset you, as you said, that's all in the past, isn't it? And everything is great now? Yes, you were adopted, but Carla, love, no need to look so sad. I mean, you've got that old house, you're young, and, I bet, well off — oh, and beautiful! Why, you could do anything you want to. What's that old saying? The world is your oyster!' And he was smiling again.

I froze, and thought again, *He doesn't understand. It's not all about things. It's the fact that I'm alone, with no past, with no family.* After a slight pause, I met his eyes and knew I must try and cheer up. He was giving me his time and spending his money on me, so I must try and be the woman he was hoping to find when he asked me out.

I made myself smile, and said, 'You're right of course, Kev. I mustn't be so silly.'

He grinned, clearly thankful that I was no longer moaning about my life. 'Another drop of wine, love?' He poured out a good half-glassful. 'Make you feel better. And now we've got a big decision — what's for pudding?'

It was a difficult choice as I had no appetite left, but in the end we both had chocolate mousse, which was delicious. Then, the wine bottle empty, and Freddie bustling around as if he wanted us to leave and so close up the little bistro, I said hesitantly, 'You must let me go halves, Kev — a lovely meal, but quite expensive ... '

A taut expression spread over his face, and he avoided my eyes as he got to his feet and came round to draw out my chair. 'No, nothing to pay, love.' He cleared his throat and I thought he looked suddenly embarrassed. 'You see, I did a job for Freddie not long ago, and he said when I wanted a good meal it would be on the house. So ... ' The grin flashed out again, and he put his arm through mine to walk me out into the street.

I was surprised. Favours for work done? Well, I supposed that was business. I got into the beautiful car, and, with my brain working hard now, asked quietly, 'So who owns this car, Kev? Another grateful customer?'

I regretted the words even before they were out. He sat beside me, giving me a long sideways stare which clearly showed he didn't like the question. He switched on the ignition. 'And if it is, what's wrong with that, then?'

I thought I heard a warning note in his voice, and at once remembered Jake's words: *Kev can be a bit nasty.* 'Sorry,' I said as lightly as possible. 'Good of whoever it is, and sorry if I spoke out of turn. I've had a nice evening, Kev, thanks very much, and I think Freddie's Bistro deserves a star or two. And now, if you wouldn't mind, can we go home? I'm a bit tired, you see.'

I wasn't sure if that was what he had in mind, but silently he took the road back to Thorn House and, stopping the car, looked at me. 'I know I'm not your sort, Carla, but I have feelings too, you know. Very sorry about your adoption, but I just want you to know I think you're great. Beautiful and smart.' His smile was warm. 'And p'raps we could go out again sometime?'

What could I say? Regret that I'd asked the wrong questions made me smile back at him. I got out of the car as quickly as I could. 'Thanks, Kev. Let's think about it, shall we? And so — well, goodnight.' I turned away and walked up the path to the house.

Indoors I locked the door, listened for the purr of the car driving away, and had a sudden feeling that home was wonderful. Safe. As if someone waited for me, smiling and saying warm, undemanding words that reassured. And I thought about what Aunt Jem had said about no ghosts, but the presences of people who had lived here long before me, and who now welcomed me back.

I sat by the red embers of a fire and drank a cup of coffee, my thoughts busy. I knew I had learned a lesson this evening. My life was of little consequence to Kev, whereas Dan had understood my misery. When I got into bed I was asleep almost instantly, feeling at home, and very happy to be so.

★   ★   ★

As soon as I was up and dressed the next morning, I thought at once of the May tree and the celebrations I must plan. I met Jake putting away his bicycle, smiled and said, 'What do you know about May Day, Jake? I want to have a real celebration on the day.'

He looked at me as if I was suddenly talking nonsense, but after a pause he frowned and said, 'Dancing round the maypole, that's what we did at school. Awful, feet always going wrong and ribbons getting twisted. But fun.'

I thought for a moment. 'I don't think we can put up a maypole, but ... hang on, didn't I once read something about welcoming back the sun after a long winter by lighting a bonfire? And burning herbs and leaping over the ashes? Did you ever hear about that?'

'Leaping over the ashes?'

I smiled and nodded. 'So I'm having a party, with lots of food and drink. And I think I'll have a big bonfire to help celebrate. You'll come, won't you, Jake?'

To my amazement, he flushed bright

pink. But he looked me in the eyes as he said, a bit unsteadily, 'Yeah, I'll be there. And … can I bring my girlfriend?'

Pleasure surged through me. 'Of course you can! The more the merrier.' I turned away, then looked back at him. 'What's she called, Jake? And is she interested in gardening?'

'Ellie,' he said, grinning, and the flush dying away. 'And no, she doesn't know a cabbage leaf from a weed, but she'll learn.'

There was so much new confidence in his voice, and such a bright expression on his face, that I felt he had received a much-needed gift. He was settling down and growing up. A job he loved and was good at; a girl to share things with.

Returning to the house, I found I was smiling, for suddenly I recognised a slight lifting of the sadness that had overwhelmed me since I'd learned I was adopted. Love, I thought, has many ways of showing itself, all of them wonderful. And then I felt a great need to see Dan, to ask him to celebrate May Day with me.

Pausing in the kitchen, I felt my heart beat a little faster as I remembered he had said we had a contract of love.

I was alive with excitement when he appeared unexpectedly in the open doorway not long after I'd thought this. His smile was like the sun shining through a dark cloud. There was so much warmth in his quiet, resonant voice as he said, 'Good morning, my love. I know it's a bit early, but I had to see you before the busy day starts at the shop. How are you?'

Instinctively I flew to him, arms wide open. There was no need to reply. I felt we were one as we savoured a long kiss. After a few breathless moments, we parted and I said huskily, 'Can you stop for a coffee? Kettle's on the boil.'

He shook his head. 'No time, I'm afraid. But we'll meet again on Saturday evening, won't we? Meriel's planning something quite sumptuous, I think. And we can see each other then.'

'How lovely,' I whispered, the thought of us being together filling my mind. And then I remembered: 'She was afraid that you might be too busy to come.'

'I'm never too busy to see you, dear love.' And I recognised the truth of those two magical words, *dear* love, spoken so quietly in his low, vibrant voice, his eyes never leaving my face.

Then he said something that sent a chill through me. It was suddenly so different from the moment we had just shared. 'I wonder if you'd be willing to let me see your aunt's manuscript, Carla? Of course, I'm sure you understand that I need to read it, to assess it, and I might be able to slide in a quiet hour this weekend, once the shop is closed.' He stopped, stepping back and looking at me. 'Would that be all right with you, my love?'

At once I said a quiet 'Yes, I'll go and fetch it,' but as I left the kitchen I knew something was wrong. Why should it suddenly be so important to read the book? Unless he had decided it must be published, and he could only get hold of it by making love to me?

Somehow I forced myself to push away the suspicious thoughts that tried to spoil the joy I had felt, and which now lingered as the day passed.

★　★　★

When Annie appeared on Friday morning, I told her about the May Day party. She grinned. 'Well, that's real good news. Asking your friends, are you? You need to have a few handy men about the place, burning branches, handing round drinks, laughing and chattering and hiding away in corners, if I know anything about them!'

We laughed together, and I felt some of the shadows that kept threatening me retreating. After all, Saturday was close, and Meriel's supper would surely bring Dan and me together, with the explanation of what I thought were his strange feelings about the book.

And so Annie and I began to plan. She looked at me keenly. 'Sausage rolls, buns with cheese and chutney, and some soup would be nice, as we're standing round the bonfire. Who's coming, then?'

I smiled at her warmly and put an arm round her in a quick hug. 'You, of course, Annie. And your husband and your neighbours — anyone you'd like to ask. And Jake will bring his girlfriend, Ellie, and … ' I paused, then went on, knowing I had to invite him. 'And his brother, Kevin. And I'm sure Meriel Fontenay and her brother will be here.'

Suddenly I could see it all happening. Flames leaping into the darkening sky. Laughter and chatter, and perhaps some antics about jumping over the fire as it died down. And the May tree watching us all, as it had watched people over the centuries celebrating its special day. Again the warm feeling of home suffused me, and I stood silently while Annie got ready to start work.

Before she left the room, she turned and said, 'Garlands — that's what you want, Carla. Always wore garlands, the people in the olden days did. Got some flowers, have you? Some wild ones, perhaps? I'll see what I can find in my garden, and we'll use those. Bend a few willow twigs, or soft hazel stems to make the bottom, see, and then stick the flowers into them. They'll look lovely.'

I heard her stumping up the stairs, but I stayed in the kitchen, my mind full of the past. The happy past that had brought me up in this ancient house. And again, the warmth spread through me as I thought of times past, and I was able to start making a grocery list, forgetting about everything except the goodies we needed to celebrate May Day.

14

On Saturday, I dressed for Meriel's supper party. I decided on the same skirt and apricot-coloured silk top that I had worn when Dan and I went out together. Perhaps if he saw me in that same outfit, it would remind him of the contract of love he had said we'd made. Perhaps it would help him to forget about Aunt Jem's book. And if only he did, then my world would be rosier, and I would feel more hopeful about the future.

But even as I took a last look at my reflection before leaving the bedroom, something made me go and take Aunt Jem's manuscript out of its hiding place and put it in my bag. No, of course I wouldn't let Dan have it. So why, then, did I feel I must take it? I didn't allow myself to think any further, but simply locked the huge door behind me and walked down the road to Meriel's house.

She greeted me with a big smile, saying, 'You look a picture! I'm glad Dan will be here. He has a soft spot for attractive women, as I'm sure you've already found out!'

I didn't trust myself to reply. If Meriel discovered that Dan and I were in love — well, we were, surely? — would she be pleased? I wondered. I followed her into the lounge, a large airy room furnished with huge leather sofas, a fireplace full of colourful foliage, and some beautiful pieces of antique furniture, all providing standing places for delicate ornaments of silver, glass and china. Old pieces, I thought admiringly; how good they looked. And then, while she suggested I sit down and then went towards the drinks cabinet, I thought back to Thorn House's old-fashioned parlour and its shabby, evocative warmth; and I knew at once which I preferred.

Soon Dan came into the room. Clearly he had been helping in the garden; now, taking off his gloves and bending to wipe some earth from his shoes, he looked at me and smiled. 'You look wonderful! I suppose I should've changed into smarter clothes — forgive me, love?' He sat on the large plum-covered sofa, close to me, and went on, 'Meriel expects some sort of payment for the meal she's spent all day preparing, so a bit of weeding seemed my fate.' He stretched his legs, thrust his arms into the air, and exhaled loudly, with an amused glance at me. 'Bad for the back, all this gardening stuff. I'll be glad to get back to books when the weekend is over.'

He slid a little nearer to me, gave me that sky-blue smile which cleared away every cloud in sight, and said gently as he took hold of my hand, 'And what have you been doing since we last met, my lovely lady?'

I was ready to tell him about the date with Kevin, but then Meriel was back, dispensing drinks, and the talk became more general. When there was a slight pause in the conversation, she looked at me. 'I've got some news about your brooch, Carla. Want to hear it now, or wait until we've had supper?'

Something jumped inside me. Aunt Jem's brooch. I longed to hear what Meriel had to tell me, so I sat up straighter and said quickly, 'I can't wait. Please go on, and tell me now.'

She sipped her drink, looking at me with those big dark eyes. 'I know I told you it might be worth a bit, but since then I met up with this chap from London who deals in Edwardian jewellery, and he nearly jumped out of his skin when he heard about that gorgeous aquamarine!'

'The aquamarine? That green-blue stone in the middle? What's so special about it?' I felt my blood begin to sing — was she going to tell me that it was worth thousands? And if she did, what on earth should I do with it?

I think she saw the confusion on my face, for at once she leaned forward and touched my arm. 'Don't worry; it's just a lovely story. You see, this chap thinks your brooch is the important missing piece of a collection of jewellery with aquamarines. An aristocrat commissioned it for his wife, and when she died the brooch disappeared. No one knows who took it — perhaps a servant, who sold it for what they could get. And so your Aunt Jem came to be the new owner — and now you!'

I relaxed in my chair. Such a lovely story, and now the brooch was safe in its hiding place upstairs at Thorn House. The story led me to believe that all its owners had thought of it with love. Aunt Jem certainly did. And now it dawned on me happily — and I smiled at Meriel — that the brooch was with another loving owner. But where would it go next?

In the short silence that filled the room now, Dan's quiet voice broke into my thoughts. 'Yes, it certainly has a history. Carla, you must wear the brooch, and let us all see its beauty.' He smiled into my eyes. 'I have a feeling that its existence is more important to you than its value, whatever that might be.'

I nodded, because words were too far away, my mind full of the past life of the brooch. I looked at Meriel. 'Would your friend, the one you were talking about, like to see the brooch, I wonder? Would it be good for him to have a look at the missing piece?'

'I'm sure he'd be absolutely delighted, Carla. But could you bear to part with it for a short while?'

I knew at once what to say. 'Yes, I'm sure it would be the right thing to let him see it, but before that I'm going to wear it at the party I'm planning for the May Day celebration.'

Meriel's smile glowed. 'What a wonderful idea! A party — and your old tree will enjoy it, I'm sure!'

I nodded. 'Yes, because in some way I think the brooch and the thorn tree and May Day are all connected.' I looked at Dan, who was sitting back, holding his empty glass and looking at me with a strange expression on his face.

'You're right, Carla,' he said. 'But you've forgotten one other link in the story, haven't you? Your aunt's manuscript?'

Of course I hadn't forgotten it, but I just nodded and tried to focus my thoughts, which were running around my mind at a terrific speed. And there were other links, too — the nylon stockings and the letters, all hiding in the Memory Box. What on earth should I do with them all?

Meriel suggested we go into the kitchen for our meal, and slowly my mind cleared. The cool colours of the airy room were pleasurable, her cooking was wonderful, and I ate the meal happily, feeling myself relaxing and sorting out the confusion inside me.

We laughed a lot during the meal, with Meriel telling tales of some of her oddest customers. 'There was this elderly Frenchman whose accent made understanding him difficult. He was looking for a book he'd read as a child, and now would pay anything to see again. No, we never did find it.' She stopped abruptly and glanced at Dan, and then at me. 'Sorry, Carla, how on earth could I mention such a thing? I mean, you have the same problem about your aunt's book, don't you? Please forgive me.'

I said, with a new feeling of certainty, 'Don't worry, Meriel. I'm not upset. In fact, what you've just told me has almost made me feel that Aunt Jem's book should certainly be published. It's wonderful to know that some people might feel like your Frenchman — ready to do almost anything to read the book.'

I looked at Dan across the table. He was smiling, his eyes alight, and I knew I had to believe in what I'd just said and so let him see the manuscript. But Meriel was clearing away our plates and chatting about how her pudding had gone a bit wrong, but she hoped we would enjoy it. And we did. It was a light-as-air sponge pudding doused with lemon and golden syrup; just the sort of thing I had enjoyed as a child with Aunt Jem. And that made it easy, once the meal was over and we decided to wander around the garden, for me to open my bag and hand the tattered manuscript to Dan, who was standing at my side.

He took it in his hands as if it were a valuable jewel, turned it over, saw the signature on the last page, and then turned back to me. His voice was low, almost inaudible, but we were alone, and I had no trouble hearing his quiet words. 'This is wonderful, Carla, my love. And you know I shall treat it with great care. I'll have the pleasure of reading it very soon — perhaps even tonight — and then I'll tell you what I think.'

We stood close together in the shadowy half-light, and I felt a great happiness rise within me. I had done what I thought was right, and much of my worry had gone. I knew that I could trust Dan with the manuscript, and I felt he would return it to me soon and say it wasn't worth publishing. And then it would go back into the Memory Box, with the letters and the other bits and pieces, and I would at last be free of anxiety about what to do with it.

I knew my smile glowed then, as I raised my face to Dan's. As we embraced, he whispered how much he loved me before he put his hands around my face, and we kissed.

He walked home with me, along the lane now full of shadows and night-time murmurs, and then we stood in the doorway of Thorn House. He looked at the old tree and grinned at me.

'So it's going to have a party, is it? Well, I look forward to it. And you'll let me help, will you, to get everything ready?'

'Yes,' I said lightly. 'But Annie will help too, and I think Jake is quite interested. And then Kevin will be there ... ' I stopped. Dan didn't know about Kev. Why had I mentioned him? I saw, in the dim light, how his expression altered. He looked at me keenly, but with amusement shining in his eyes.

'And who is Kev? I haven't heard about him. Not a potential suitor, I hope?'

'Of course not. He's Jake's brother, and he asked me out one evening.'

Dan put his arms around me and said into my hair, 'I don't want you to have other boyfriends. I want you to be mine alone, Carla — I love you so much.'

For a moment I paused, wondering what to say. It was wonderful to be loved, of course, but I knew that an as independent woman I needed to live my life without any restraints. Slowly I eased out of his arms. 'Don't be silly, Dan — when I love someone it'll be him alone. I don't intend to have a long line of possible lovers!'

Then he smiled, and his voice was full of laughter. 'Thank goodness for that! And now I must leave you. Sweet dreams, my love, and I'll see you again very soon.'

'Yes, and when you've read the book you must tell me what you think.'

We kissed again and then parted. He walked past the thorn tree, and I saw a branch catch on his jacket. But only for a moment. He released it, and then disappeared down the path, on his way back to Meriel's house.

I unlocked the door and went into the calm quietness of Thorn House. All I could think of was that I had given Dan Aunt Jem's manuscript. And now the thorn tree catching on his jacket brought fresh doubt into my mind. Could it possibly be suggesting I had done the wrong thing?

15

The next day I had a phone call from Kev. 'Hi there, lovely girl,' he said. 'Do me a favour, will you?'

Cautiously I said, 'Not before I know what it is. Details, please.'

A loud laugh echoed down the line, nearly deafening me. 'OK, OK, no need to get uppity. I simply want your company when I go to the garden centre. Jake's birthday is coming up, see, and I need advice about what to get him. I thought maybe one of those light modern wheelbarrows that fold up — what do you think?'

I considered for a moment. I was glad Kev was ready to give his brother a present. But — a wheelbarrow? Surely mine, which he was using, had a bit more life in it?

I stuttered a bit, but Kev's mind was clearly made up, as he said, 'Your old thing is pretty useless — I should bin it.'

'All right, Kev, I'll come. And yes, I might just buy a few pot plants, ready for the party.'

'Party? What's that, then? Inviting me, are you?'

I could see I had no option but to answer, with a laugh, 'Of course I am! It's next week, on May Day, the first of the month, and I want to celebrate the old tree.'

'What, that prickly old bush growing all over your wall?' He chortled, and I had a sudden feeling of having to stand up for the thorn tree.

I said curtly, 'It's a May tree, not just a bush, and I'm intending to celebrate it. But you don't have to come if you don't want to.'

His voice became gentler. 'Oh, don't be like that, Carla. Of course I want to come. And I might even send that awful old bush a birthday card. But what about going to the garden centre? Pick you up about two-ish? That be all right?'

I said yes. Kev was a bit of clown, but

giving Jake a wheelbarrow showed his heart was in the right place. I would make sure he chose the right sort, and we could talk about the party afterwards. Suddenly it was cheering to think I might see him again, and so soon.

*   *   *

The garden centre was humming with customers, and we had to ask where the wheelbarrows were. Kevin picked one up and wheeled it up and down for a moment. Then he looked at me and grinned. 'See me doing this in old age, can you? When I've retired and want to grow veg?'

'Quite honestly, no. I can't you sitting about and not doing much.'

He put down the barrow, looked at it again, and then said, turning back to me, 'You got me right, haven't you, love? Not the settling-down sort, me. Guess I'll be on me travels somewhere when old age comes along.'

I nodded. He was a rolling stone, and unlike me, had no intention of living quietly in the country in his old age. I wasn't really disappointed, because I knew it was Dan who I loved. But what he had just said proved that I needn't accompany him on any more dates. Better for him to find a woman who viewed the future as he did, I thought. And then I was smiling, for a small shadow had just lifted from my mind. No more worries about Kev always asking me out.

I left him to take the wheelbarrow to an assistant; then, grinning, I asked for it to be gift-wrapped. 'Gift-wrapped?' the assistant said, amazed.

Kev gave her one his charming smiles and said airily, 'Money's no object, love. Just do it, will you?'

I felt so good about all this that I went off and found a selection of pot plants, most of them in bud and showing bits of promising colour. I looked carefully, visualising where they would stand in my garden, and the image came of two or three beneath the thorn tree — a delicate white daisy with fronded leaves, and a rich scarlet begonia which would reflect the touch of red in the centre of the thorn flowers when they burst out into full bloom.

We left the garden centre, both of us pleased with our purchases, and Kev full of amusement as he said, 'Guess young Jake'll wonder what on earth I'm giving him.' As we drove back we smiled at each other, and I thought how good it was that I could now think of Kev as a rather wild friend, no longer someone who wanted so badly to take me out.

Getting out of the van and watching him carry my pots up the path to the house, I said, 'Thanks, Kev. And remember, the party is on May Day — next week, on the first. Make sure you're here, won't you? I shall need some help with the bonfire.'

He stared at me. 'Bonfire? Oh well, if that's what turns you on, love. See you next week, then. Cheers for now.' And he was off, the white van rattling over the rough path and then roaring down the lane.

Carefully, I placed my two new pots

at the foot of the thorn tree and smiled at it. 'Making you pretty for your day,' I said, and then thought what a sentimental fool I was.

I went indoors and sat down, making plans. Burgers, sausage rolls, cheese rolls, homemade soup, some rich creamy goodies to follow, and something to wash it all down with. Coffee, and what else? Cider, I thought, and knew I must talk to Annie about this. Would her farmer nephew be able to produce some? By tea time I was ablaze with plans and images, and I knew it was going to be a wonderful day.

Dan phoned in the late afternoon. 'How are you, my love?' His voice was quiet and tender, and I felt warmth run through me.

'I'm fine,' I said, and smiled as I realised our love contract was still going strong. I wanted badly to ask him if he'd read Aunt Jem's manuscript, but somehow the words wouldn't come. And anyway, he was telling me about the book fair up country where he had to go tomorrow. I thought about another day of not seeing him, and my smile faded. But he was unexpectedly asking me to go with him.

'It'll be a lot of fun,' he said. 'Interesting people, authors talking about their books, good food, sitting in a sunny field — what more could you want?'

I paused a moment, then asked, 'How long will you be there, Dan? And are you driving up?' I thought at first that it might be lovely to go to a new place with Dan and listen to some book talks, but then I realised I was too busy at Thorn House to leave it now.

He sounded disappointed. 'You don't want to come? I thought we might stay in a pub up there. Yes, I'm driving up, and I remember from last year that it's a spectacular journey — masses of trees and daffodils just coming out on the road verges.' His voice quietened. 'Say you'll come, Carla? I can't think of anything nicer than you and me together on an interesting jaunt.'

I considered. Yes, it would be lovely, driving in the sun and meeting new people, and Dan and I sharing it all. But then words came out before I could stop them. 'Well, going off on a jaunt, as you call it, must mean you're not quite so busy as you thought.' I stopped, but out it came, a bit sharp and unstoppable. 'Dan, have you had a chance to read Aunt Jem's manuscript?'

There was a lengthening pause, and I held my breath. *I shouldn't have been so impatient and unloving.* 'Sorry, Dan. I didn't mean to sound like that — just that it's on my mind, wondering what you thought of it.'

Now it was he who paused before answering. 'I do understand, love, but I really have been terribly busy today in the shop. More customers than usual, and all wanting help to find their books. Then I've had to find time to talk with visiting reps. No, Carla, love, I haven't read it yet. But I will, of course, I promise you, so try and wait a bit longer, will you?'

I swallowed the lump in my throat and finally said, 'Yes, I understand. But it's so important to me. Well, when you come home again, I'm sure you'll read it. And no thanks, but I haven't the time to go away this weekend. I'm trying to get everything ready for the May Day party, you see.'

I'd run out of words and excuses, and listened miserably while he said, his voice a little tenser than usual, 'Yes, I see. Don't worry about it, love. And don't work too hard — I'm looking forward to the party. When is it, on the first day of the month? Well I'll certainly be back by then.'

Wearily, I just said, 'Yes, and have a good time, Dan. I'll look forward to your return. So until then, well, goodbye.' I clicked off the phone, feeling anxious and uncertain about our so-called contract of love. Was it coming to an unloving end? And did Dan feel as bad as I did? Unhappily, I looked into the future, and wondered if I should go back to my enjoyable job in London. If I did, then Thorn House must be let to some strangers, and I wouldn't live there any longer. Was that I what wanted? I just didn't know.

It was later in the evening when a tap on the kitchen door brought a smiling Meriel into my gloomy life. 'Evening!' she said lightly. 'I was told to come and cheer you up. So what about a coffee or something? Shall I put the kettle on?'

I gaped at her. 'What on earth? What do you mean? Who told you I needed cheering up? And yes, I'll put the kettle on at once.'

She sat down, still smiling, and talked lightly about her garden, her antiques, her step-brother driving off to goodness knew where, and what a bore he was with his books. And then, as I poured the coffee and offered the biscuit tin, she looked at me more seriously, the smile disappearing; and a strange, rather veiled expression made her look half-asleep.

She took a biscuit and then looked at me. 'One of my odd times, Carla. I was suddenly aware of something wrong at Thorn House. I knew I must come and try to sort it out.'

I held my breath for a long moment. *Something wrong at Thorn House.* Suddenly I knew she was right. *I* was what was wrong with Thorn House. Me and my worries about the wretched manuscript, with fears that Dan might not love me after all, and perhaps I should leave the old house and start a new life somewhere else.

We looked at each other, and for a moment I felt the house vibrating, full of something that instinctively I knew I could not leave — presences from the past, warmth, safety, and most of all, love. I took in a deep breath and met Meriel's eyes, unveiled now and looking at me with great interest. I said quietly, 'I can't thank you enough for that. You've solved everything. Yes, I can think much clearer now. I don't know how you do it, but yes, you were right. I certainly did need cheering up, and you've done it!'

We looked at each other and smiled, and I realised what a true friend she was. I pushed the biscuit tin over to her again and said, 'More coffee? And perhaps this is the time to talk about the May Day celebrations?'

'I've been talking to Annie about old customs,' Meriel said, 'and it appears that we should wear garlands of flowers. Well, I know a chap who sells wonderful cut flowers in the market — what about me buying quite a few bunches, and then putting them together with whatever garden and wildflowers we can find?'

She looked quite excited at the thought of all these wonderful garlands we must wear, and I said at once, 'Well, Meriel, that's a marvellous thought. And thank you so much — I'll come with you to the market and help carry them all home. And then we've got to put them together, haven't we?'

She nodded, and I saw the sparkle in her eyes was still there. 'Better than garlands, Carla — I thought we'd make posies for everyone. I feel that the old thorn would like that.'

When the coffee was finished, and we were back to talking about more plans for May Day, I said, 'Let's go into the garden, shall we? This is such a lovely time of day, all warm and glowing, even as the colours fade.'

We went out, stopping by the thorn tree and looking at it. Meriel said seriously, 'Try and remember, Carla, just what things this old tree has seen — excitement, fear, tragedy and happiness; and how it lives on, no matter what happens in this house.'

I walked down the path with her, said a warm goodbye, and then went back to the kitchen, and finally up to bed. I thought about all she had said, and realised the truth of those extraordinary words.

16

So much to think about, and to do. I woke up early, briskly got dressed, and walked round the garden before breakfast. Jake was doing a grand job. As well as caring for his veg plants and the small seedlings, which were growing fast, he had found time to look at my summer border and tidy it up.

I perched on an old wooden bench that had seen better days and smiled, remembering. Aunt Jem and I had often had our tea out here after her afternoon stint of writing. I had been trying to master the latest maths problem set for homework and not succeeding very well. But once we were eating our way through new scones, jam and cream, and I listened to her telling me about her stories, somehow life had become more comfortable. We talked also about flowers and what would fit into that space below the beech hedge, and also which shrub must be pruned once it had finished flowering. Scraps of conversation now came back to me, banishing my worries, and filling my mind with happy memories.

Gratitude had been part of those talks; Aunt Jem was grateful for her talent, and, I thought now, of having adopted a child who was proving to be all she ever wanted. She didn't talk about her past; and as I sat here now, the letters between her and her sister, Millie, who I had thought to be my mother, came to my mind. And with them came a new understanding — that there was no need to keep these tattered bits of scribbled paper, for that life was all gone. I was here, now, with a different sort of life to deal with. Wouldn't it be sensible to do away with them, allowing their unhappiness and unfulfilled longing for children to rest in peace? For I was here, one child at least who had brought Aunt Jem all that she had ever wanted.

I heard Jake locking his bike, and got up. Goodness, it was long past breakfast time. As we exchanged good mornings and some comments on the weather and growing plants, I knew that in some strange way I was moving on. And it was a wonderful feeling, for I knew very certainly that the future waited for me; a future of content and possible happiness. Even the worry about Dan and Aunt Jem's book was gone.

I went indoors and made coffee and a bit of toast, and then made my plans for the day. I went shopping, taking my list with me, and returned with everything I would need for the coming party. Then I sat still and told myself I needed something suitable to wear on May Day. Jeans and a well-worn T-shirt wouldn't do. The thorn tree demanded a best dress. Yes, I thought happily — I would buy something new and amazing with which to greet my visitors and make merry. Something that perhaps the thorn tree would like. Laughing at such silly thoughts, I found myself hoping that Dan would like it too, and that everything would be happy on the great day of celebration.

I found just what I was hoping to find in a little newly opened boutique up a side street in town. It was made of a greeny-blue linen, smooth and form-fitting, with small shoulder straps that I imagined would carry the aquamarine brooch very comfortably. The girl serving me said, 'Looks wonderful. Are you going to a party or something?'

I smiled and simply said, 'Yes. And it's a lovely dress; thanks for helping me choose it.'

Then I left and headed for Dan's bookshop. I knew he wouldn't be there, of course, but I was pretty sure Lily would make coffee while I chose a gardening book for Jake's birthday. Something else whispered in my mind as I walked along. *Instinct*, I thought. *Never ignore it. But let's hope it brings good news, not bad.*

Lily was busy with a small group of people when I arrived, but she glanced across at me and nodded her head towards one of the chairs set around the room. So I sat down and waited. We would have a chat when she was free. I wanted her to tell me a bit more about Dan — what he was like to work for, and all the little things that go towards really getting to know someone.

When finally the shop was empty again, she went towards the kitchen, saying as she went, 'I'll get us some coffee. All right for Dan to go off on one if his many book fairs, but I'm left with the business on my hands.' I thought her smile wasn't as pleasant as usual. Over her shoulder, as she went into the kitchen, she said, 'I need a break after coping with that lot. And then I want to talk to you.'

That surprised me. What on earth could Lily and I have in common? Then it struck me that Dan had told me she was his partner in the business, his co-director. I had thought she was just an assistant, but apparently she was much more. And whatever did she want to talk to me about?

I picked up a magazine on the table next to me, but couldn't concentrate. Something was worrying me, and all the old uneasiness came flooding back. Dan, Aunt Jem's manuscript, the sad letters and the brooch ... and I had thought it was all over. Just me and Dan, and Thorn House. Now I had the feeling it wasn't like that at all.

Lily returned with a tray of coffee and biscuits. She seated herself opposite me and looked at me with clear hazel eyes. 'Well,' she said, her voice crisp and business-like, 'I have news for you about Jemima Marshall's old manuscript. Good news, actually. You see, I've found a publisher who's read it and is full of praise. He wants to buy the copyright and get it into print as soon as he can. So tell me what you think of that.'

What did I think? Only that my mind was suddenly awhirl. Dan must have read the book and then gone ahead with sending it to possible publishers, without telling me. And yet, how well I remember his gentle voice reassuring me that he would never do anything without my consent and understanding. And now it was all settled. The book was coming into print. Revealing all my secrets. And all without a word to me.

I could only shake my head and stare at Lily. 'He said he wouldn't do anything without my consent,' I whispered at last, and was surprised when her only reaction was to laugh.

'You don't understand booksellers, do you, Carla? An ambitious lot, and I have to tell you that Dan is the same. Perhaps not as bad as others I could name, but for all that, he's obsessive about his book business.' She pushed the plate of biscuits across the table. I didn't take one. It would choke me, I knew.

I just looked at her, and then words came from deep within me. 'And when did Dan have time to read the manuscript?' I asked her. 'When I gave it to him, he said he'd read it after work that same day. So did he, but then didn't tell me what he intended to do? I want the truth, Lily.'

She didn't reply at once, and I thought a look of uneasiness spread across her lovely face. Then she said, 'Actually, he didn't read it. We were too busy in the shop for him to find the time. So when I found it beneath the counter in his locked drawer, I unlocked it and read it myself.'

'*You* read it?' My breath came out in a huge gasp.

She had the grace to look slightly embarrassed before saying quickly, 'Well, I am a co-director, you know. I have just the same rights that Dan has to send possible books to a publisher.' Her voice rose slightly. 'And he was away, having fun at his wretched book fair, and so ...'

I cut in, anger getting the better of me. 'And so you thought you'd something to please yourself. Have you told Dan? He has a phone, you know.'

She ran a hand through her shining hair. 'No, I haven't. I wanted it all sealed and signed before he comes back. He'll be pleased, of course.'

A new, gentler feeling crept over me. It was no good blaming this wretched, self-seeking, ambitious woman. And what was the point of blaming Dan for not reading the manuscript first? He was too busy — yes, I could understand that. And locking the manuscript in his private drawer? No doubt he planned to read it first thing on his return to the bookshop, and then talk to me, as he had promised.

I sat back in my chair, slowly drank the cooling coffee, and then said purposefully, 'Lily, please give me the phone number of the publisher who has the manuscript. I want to talk to them and tell them it's all a mistake. I never wanted it to be published. I'm sure they'll understand.'

Lily looked at me and smiled, and there was pleasure in her voice as she said, 'Sorry, Carla, can't do that. I'm afraid you'll have to wait until Dan is back. And also, I don't understand why you're so angry about the book going into print. Whatever is the reason? I'm sure it'll sell very well and make you a ton of money.' She continued to look at me, and her smile grew broader. 'What a funny creature you are. I don't understand, either, why you think Dan has any feelings for you — except, of course, being successful with your late aunt's final book.'

I knew that if I didn't get up and go, I should end by flinging my empty coffee cup at her. So I pushed back my chair and walked straight towards the door. Then I turned and gave her a last, despairing stare. 'You'd never understand how I feel about this book, Lily. You see, you just don't have the heart to understand all that's going through my mind. But Dan does. And I think he'll understand how I feel now, when I see him again. Sorry, Lily, but I have to go now.' I walked out the door, along the street and towards the car park, my thoughts circling until I almost felt dizzy.

But in the car I felt reality hit me as I drove back towards Thorn House. I had had the biggest and worst shock of my life. And also — I managed a slight smile — I had quite forgotten to buy a birthday present for Jake.

Thorn House — home — was waiting for me. The huge front door opened with its usual squeak, but I imagined it was a welcome. It had always been there, and as I went upstairs to unpack the new dress and hang it up, I was back in the past, thinking of all the emotions that the old May tree had shared with the people who had lived here. Not just Aunt Jem and her urgent longing for a child, which she knew would never be fulfilled. Great sadness there. But perhaps when she decided to adopt, there would have been excitement. Did she tell anyone else of her decision? And then when she had chosen me and brought me here to live a new life in my new home, there might have been anxiety about whether it was all going to work out. Obviously she had confided her secret to her old maid, Bertha, who had comforted her.

And then I had no doubt that a great peace of mind had slowly filled her, offering another chance to finish the story in her series of children's books. She had watched me grow, and been delighted when my job in London proved satisfying. So life had gone on. But had she ever thought of what would happen when she was no longer in Thorn House? Well, of course she had done. She left the old house to me, her chosen child. This last thought proved to be just what I had been searching for: the reassurance that even though my emotions were in turmoil, I knew I was doing the right thing; doing what she had hoped I would do — living in Thorn House and enjoying my life.

Until now. Rapidly the past faded away, and in my mind I was once again glaring at Lily and wondering how Dan could ever have let me down in this horrible way. I must speak to him, tell him what I thought of him, and say very strongly that he must get the book away from the publisher. Soon. I went downstairs and picked up my phone.

He answered after a couple of rings, his voice music to my ears; but even so, it was unable to dissolve the rage that filled me. I shouted down the phone. 'Dan, Lily has played a terrible trick on me. You must tell the publisher that I won't have the book printed. You must come back and tell them at once.'

There was a moment's silence while

my heavy breathing subsided. Then Dan replied quietly, but with a steely note in his voice, 'I don't know what you're talking about, love. Calm down, will you, and tell me just what's happened?'

By now the rage had begun to fade, and I felt myself trying to be more reasonable; to put everything into understandable words. But suddenly I was crying, great sobs that made it hard to breathe. And Dan was saying anxiously, 'Carla, whatever's the matter? For goodness sake, tell me.'

But I had no words. All I could do was whisper through my sobs, 'But I thought you loved me,' and then I clumsily switched off the phone.

17

Hardly knowing what I was doing, I walked rapidly down to Meriel's house, and found her busily unpacking a box of small, beautiful miniature paintings. She waved me to a chair and then pushed one of them across the table, saying, 'Look at this. He was a young man who displeased the queen in Tudor times, got sent to the Tower, and then was executed. But here he's smiling.'

I picked it up. It was delicate and very real-looking. I handed it back to her, saying quietly, 'How very sad. But, yes, he's smiling.'

Meriel packed up the miniatures again and then looked at me across the table, saying gently, 'Which is what you must do, Carla.' She paused. 'I don't know what's happened, but it's all in your face, and I want to help you to get over it.'

I nodded. 'It's Dan,' I said. 'And Aunt

Jem's book. And I'm so unhappy about it all. What should I do, Meriel?'

'First of all, have a cup of coffee, and then tell me all about it. Hang on while I do the coffee.' She disappeared into the kitchen, taking the box of antiques with her. I thought about the young, smiling face I had just admired, and thought of what she had said — that smiling was what I should be doing. I put my face in my hands and thought wretchedly, *How can I smile when my whole life has turned upside down and I don't know what to do next?*

But when she returned with a tray and poured me a good strong coffee, I was able to meet her questioning eyes and say feebly, 'Smiling is very hard, Meriel. But yes, I'll try and see what I can do.' I forced my face into a happy expression, which somehow helped me to feel more cheerful.

'That's more like it, Carla. And now tell me the whole story.'

So I did, telling her everything. That I was adopted, and had been shocked when I learned the truth, having read Aunt Jem's manuscript, with its gentle hints that I could be the heroine. Shocked even though she had told me lovingly that I was her chosen child, the child she had been longing for ever since her love affair had gone wrong. And then I told Meriel about not wanting the book to be published because the world would know that I was an orphan with an unknown background. And that made me feel awful — for who was I, really?

She smiled so reassuringly when I'd finished that I managed a vague sort of smile, adding, 'I know you must think I'm just a weak misery, but Meriel, that's how I feel.' I stopped, my mind suddenly visualising Dan, hearing his voice, feeling his kiss; and then I couldn't stop the last secret words erupting. 'Dan said — said — that he loves me. That we have a contract of love. And now he's broken it, and I'm left without anyone in my life who loves me.' I was ready to weep again, but Meriel's clear voice stopped me.

'I never heard such nonsense,' she said.

'You're just feeling sorry for yourself, when you have so many things to do and to look forward to. And as for Dan not loving you anymore, that's ridiculous. I know he loves you. I've seen it in his eyes. And just because he's made one mistake, you tell yourself you don't love him anymore. Wake up, Carla, for goodness sake! Life isn't all pain and misery, you know!'

I stared at her, instantly full of mixed feelings. She hadn't believed me! She was telling me foolish things that meant nothing. Or did they? Very slowly I let them run around my mind, and then I found that I was able to smile properly. To look at her and say, almost in a whisper, 'Thank you, Meriel. You're right, of course, like you always are. Yes, I am a person in my own right. I am Carla Marshall, with so much to be grateful for. The old house that I feel is my home; enough money to live on, with a job in London if I need to go back to it; and you as my friend.'

'And don't forget Annie Grey. And Jake, and that bothering brother of his.

And Dan, the most loving of them all. You have so much love in your life, Carla. Just be grateful for all of it.'

* * *

It was only later, after I had gone home, that I realised the truth of those wise words. They helped me to assess my life, but could do nothing to remove my anger at what Lily had done. Nor could I stop the horrible thought that Dan had been complicit in the arrangements with the publisher, despite being away from the bookshop.

By bedtime I was feeling sore and hurt as well as disappointed. I remembered what Meriel had said, and managed to feel grateful for all I had, but this business about the book had cut a deep wound in my wild emotions. Before I finally slept, I wondered what would happen next. I needed desperately to see Dan, but he was probably still away. And what about our contract of love? I drifted off to sleep, and my last thought was that he had broken that contract.

It must have been about two or three o'clock when I heard the noise. It broke into my dreams, and I sat up, heart thumping. I knew it was a car coming to a halt in the drive. There were rapid footsteps on the noisy gravel, and then a huge resounding couple of knocks on the front door.

I had no idea who this could be, coming here in the middle of the night and filling me with alarm. I got up, crept to the window, and looked down, but saw nothing. Again that loud knock on the door. And then, like a storm of hail, small stones hitting the window next to where I stood. And a voice, calling me.

'Carla, wake up. I have to talk to you. Carla ...'

Dan. Here, now, his voice peremptory and resonant. I felt a mixture of emotions spread through me as I pulled on a dressing gown and went down the dark stairs. I opened the front door, and he stood before me.

'Carla,' he said again, but now his voice

was full of relief, and a warmer note banished my fright.

'What on earth are you doing here? I thought you were away over the weekend.' I heard the tremble in my quick words, and wondered what to do next — whether to greet him with open arms, or say coldly that I would prefer to talk the next day; that I wanted to go back to bed, so would he please leave?

But then his arms were around me, the warmth of his body telling me that I wasn't dreaming. This was real. But so were my emotions, so ragged and painful. Even as he bent his head to kiss me, I pulled away. How dare he behave as if nothing had changed?

'No,' I said huskily. 'Don't pretend it's all right again. You know it isn't, because you know what you've done — you and Lily.' I turned and raced up the stairs, leaving him there in the hall, staring after me, but not calling after me as I thought he would.

I was back in the bedroom, shaking with emotion, when his voice reached me from the hall. 'I don't know what you mean, Carla. What has Lily got to do with anything between us?'

I shook my head, but made no answer. And then I heard him again, determined, full of steel. 'I'll sort all this out and then I'll be back. Sometime tomorrow. Go to sleep, Carla. Goodnight, my love.'

I got into bed, heard him drive away, and listened wildly to the night sounds: a bird twittering as dawn broke; the old house shifting on its timbers. But there was no one here to comfort me. I lay for what seemed a long time, thinking, wondering, but at last drifted off to sleep. And when I woke the next morning, it was to find I was still thinking the same thoughts — Dan, the book, Lily, the all-important publisher; and, most urgent of all, the fact that I was adopted. Nothing, it seemed, would ever heal that particular wound.

But I forced myself to try and live my normal life. Get up, dress, make some breakfast, welcome Jake, and then ... The telephone rang.

It was Meriel, her voice urgent. 'Carla, are you all right? Dan just phoned me saying something about problems over your Aunt Jem's book. He wouldn't tell me exactly what it was, but he said he wanted me to contact you. He thought you needed to talk to someone.'

I said nothing for a moment, but felt a great comfort spread over me. 'Yes,' I said unsteadily, 'I do need to talk, Meriel. Can you come around this morning?'

'I'll be with you in ten minutes. Put the kettle on — I think strong coffee is called for. All right, Carla? See you soon.' And she was gone.

She came, just as she had said, in ten minutes, by which time I had made coffee and opened the biscuit tin. I was delighted to see her. Sensible, intuitive Meriel would put me right, I was sure. She was smiling, and, putting the basket she carried on the floor beside her chair, she said at once, 'Look — I've brought what flowers I could find. I thought we could get busy making small posies ready for the great day. What do you say?'

'What?' My mind didn't seem to be working properly, but I tried to concentrate. 'The flowers? The great day? Meriel, I don't know ... '

'What I'm talking about? Let me enlighten you. Friday is May Day, and we agreed to make posies for everyone to wear. So I thought we'd get cracking this morning. Have you time to help me?'

Slowly my mind began to work properly. May Day — Friday. The flowers for everybody to wear at the party. The party! My new dress, with Aunt Jem's aquamarine brooch shining proudly on my shoulder. Suddenly I was my old self. Excitement filled me now, and I smiled at Meriel through tear-filled eyes. 'You must think me an absolute idiot! Of course we'll make the posies. Let me see your flowers.'

She pushed the basket towards me, and I saw the way she looked at me. *Kind,* I thought. *So wise, and — yes, loving.* And then it hit me — shame for behaving like a spoiled child denied a treat. Shame for treating Dan so badly. For what I had said to Lily. Even the issue of my adoption retreated into the background. I didn't imagine it was gone for good, but relief spread through me, for I had friends, and they would all help me. And yes, we had a party coming up!

When we'd finished our coffee, Meriel put the flowers on the table between us, producing scissors, some florist's wire, and a supply of frondy foliage. I said, 'These are lovely — and you must have stripped your garden picking them all.'

She took two small flowers, one a pale pink daisy and the other a bright blue spiky flower head, and then put a couple of leaves with them. 'I think three flowers will do, and the leaves. And no, Carla, the garden isn't quite empty. Remember it's spring, and everything is growing at a tremendous rate. The flowerbeds will soon be full of colour and life again. Look, this is how I suggest we make the posies.' Her clever fingers fiddled with the wire, and then there was a beautiful little bunch that I could see someone wearing with pleasure.

'That's amazing,' I said humbly. 'Here, let me see if can do one like it.'

The morning seemed so much brighter and happier than I had imagined it could be. I told her the story of Lily arranging with a publisher to have Aunt Jem's book put into print against my will, and ended by adding in a broken voice, 'And I was awful to Dan. I think I've hurt him deeply.'

Meriel put down the bunch she was fiddling with and smiled at me. 'Serves him right, Carla, if he really has betrayed you like this. But it sounds to me more like Lily getting up to her tricks — which wouldn't be the first time. And don't worry about Dan. He's a strong man, and he'll be back before very long.'

I looked at her suddenly misty eyes, and whispered, 'How do you know that?'

'It's the old witch thing I told you about.' She grinned. 'Oh yes, I know everything will work out in the end.'

The door opened after a short knock, and there stood Annie Grey, unbuttoning her cardigan and saying, 'Chap outside wants a word, Carla. Jake's brother, I think. Shall I tell him to come in?'

18

I gave Meriel a quick look, and I'm sure she must have seen my irritation. But she just smiled and nodded as she made another posy. So I said, 'Yes, of course, Annie.'

Kev, dressed for work, stepped into the kitchen. He looked a bit embarrassed, I thought, but he gave me one of his big grins and said, 'I'm going up the road for a job, so thought I'd just pop in while I was passing. About tomorrow, see … '

'What about tomorrow, then? I invited you to the party, didn't I?' Really, I thought, I could do without Kev bothering me. But I returned his smile, and then saw how his broadened until he looked really pleased with himself. 'Well?' I continued.

He shuffled a bit and then said, 'It's Jake's birthday, see? Same day as your party. And so I wondered … '

'Wondered what, Kev? Come on, tell me.' I knew I sounded impatient, but I was keen to get on with the posies.

'I've made him a cake. Wondered if I could bring it along, and we could celebrate his birthday as well as your old May tree.'

I was amazed. So Kev made cakes! For a moment I wondered what it would be — a creamy sponge, or perhaps a solid fruit cake? I smiled and said, 'What a lovely idea! Of course you must bring it. And oh goodness, that reminds me — I didn't get Jake the book I was thinking about for his birthday.' My smile died as yesterday flashed through my mind — most of all, Dan's betrayal with the manuscript.

Meriel came to the rescue. 'Still plenty of time,' she said brightly. 'Why not go to the shop this afternoon? Maybe you'll be able to have a talk with Dan. I know he's there all day.' She caught my eye and gave me one of her firm smiles, and then turned to look at Kev, who was standing beside the table looking rather uncertain.

'Here,' she said, and handed him a small white rose from the basket of flowers. 'That'll bring a smile to your face, Kevin. And I must tell you that the work you did in my kitchen is proving excellent. You're a good chap.'

For a second or two Kev looked amazed, and seemed speechless. Then the famous great grin spread across his face again as he took the flower and tucked it into the top buttonhole of his jacket. 'Thanks, Mrs Fontenay. Reckon I'll smell nice all day now! Well, better be on my way. And, Carla, I'll see you tomorrow after work, and I'll bring the cake with me. Cheers then, Mrs Fontenay, Carla.' And he was gone, footsteps crunching down the gravel path, and then the old van spluttered into life as he drove away.

By now Annie was ready to start work. But before she went upstairs with her box of cleaning gear, she looked at me. 'Him make a cake? Better have some indigestion pills ready, I'd say!'

Meriel and I looked at each other, and then we both burst out laughing. Then she said lightly, 'Well, it's good to see you laughing again, Carla. So what about my idea of going to the shop this afternoon and talking things over with Dan? And you said something about buying a book for Jake, didn't you?'

For a moment I sat quietly, her wise words clearing my brain and helping me to think properly. How right she was. Of course I must find Dan and try and sort out this awful muddle. I would go to the bookshop this afternoon.

'Good idea, Meriel, and thanks very much. I'll definitely go. But now we must finish these posies.' So we sat there, arranging flowers and leaves and quietly chatting about other things; about Aunt Jem's brooch, my new dress, and how I had great plans for the party on Friday. 'I want the old May tree to understand that we're glad it's here. Is that stupid, or what?'

I looked at her, expecting laughter, but she clearly understood. 'Marvellous idea. And I bet it'll enjoy the party as much as all of us will.'

At last the final little bunch was finished, and the whole lot put carefully into a big jug of water to keep fresh until we distributed them tomorrow. 'Will you stay for lunch, Meriel?' I asked as she picked up the basket and walked towards the open door.

She smiled. 'No thanks, Carla. I must get home. Who knows how many messages are waiting for me? I forget I have a business to run as well as fiddling around with flowers. See you tomorrow evening — and good luck with your talk to Dan this afternoon.' She turned before leaving, and her smile was gone. 'Don't let him get away with anything. Remember, you have your own life to lead. Well, cheerio, then.' And she was away.

I was stirring soup when Anne appeared, put away her cleaning gear, and then looked at me and gave me that same old sly, gossipy smile that appeared so easily. 'Well,' she said, doing up her cardigan buttons, 'a little bird tells me that things aren't going well for you, maid. In love with him, were you? Oh well, plenty of fresh fish in the sea, you know!'

Before I could say the shocked words that ran into my mind, she was grinning again and going through the doorway. 'I'll bring you some more of they old posies tomorrow,' she added, 'along with something to eat at your party. And a small barrel of cider. Cheer up, maid — we all have ups and downs, you know. Fingers crossed that yours will soon be over and everything right again. Cheerio, Carla.' And off she went.

I ate the soup with a roll and butter, all the reassuring words I'd heard that morning resounding in my mind. By the time I'd finished and cleared away, I knew that the afternoon was going to be a challenge, and I just hoped I would feel all the better when it was over.

* * *

The door of the bookshop was open, and I saw a few customers looking around the shelves. Nervously I went in, telling myself that I felt calm and knew exactly what

I would say to Dan. But when suddenly he was beside me, looking at me with his penetrating eyes, and a gentle smile but also an expression of slight anxiety on his lean, angled face, I forgot the words I had prepared.

'Carla, my love.' His resonant voice was low, but the warmth of it once again captivated me.

'Oh Dan,' I whispered, 'thank goodness you're here. We have to talk.'

Taking my hand, he led me into the small back room where the coffee machine and rows of teacups stood, and pulled out a couple of chairs. 'Sit down, my love. Lily's out on an errand, but she'll be back soon. In the meantime, let's hope we won't be interrupted by too many customers coming in.' He sat beside me and leaned close. 'Now, I've got your aunt's manuscript back. I drove off very early this morning to collect it. And then I read it.'

I took a deep breath. 'You've got it back! That's wonderful, Dan. And … ' I hesitated. 'What did you think of it?'

He took my hands. His were strong and hard, but I knew they were loving. 'It's a very good story, Carla. The publisher is keen to put it in the series of children's books your aunt published. There'd be a new title for the whole series, which would be published in three books.' His smile broadened. 'Of course, they hope to give it some good publicity, so that it'll catch the Christmas market. My love, it just needs one word from you.' He looked into my wide, surprised eyes with such intensity that for a moment I couldn't think what to say.

A three-book series to sell and delight more children! But then, out of the back of my mind, the old fear returned. I said, with a catch in my voice, 'Yes, that's wonderful news, Dan. But it doesn't help me with my problem, does it?'

He stroked my hands. 'You mean because you're afraid that you'll be discovered to be the actual heroine? But that's ridiculous, love. And, anyway, if it did happen, surely by now your adoption is no trouble to you?'

All I could do was shake my head and try and stop the threatening tears. I blinked hard, and then heard his quiet, wonderful words which made my heart leap.

'Carla, my love, you must remember that you were your aunt's chosen child. She loved you as if you were her own, as you told me. So what's all this sadness filling you up? Tell me, please. I want to help. You see, I love you very much.'

Through misty eyes, I met his own, loving and hopeful. Suddenly heard myself ask, a little tremulously, 'Do you mean that — that our contract of love is still there between us, Dan?'

He leaned closer, and I thought he would kiss me, for I could see the need in his face — but suddenly the door opened and Lily came in. 'Hallo, she said brightly. 'Getting our new client all excited, are you, Dan? I'm so glad I took it upon myself to send that bundle of old paper off when I did.' She glanced at her watch. 'Coffee time, I think, and here come the customers.'

Dan got up, looking anxiously down at me, and I knew I had to make an effort and reassure him. I said quickly, 'I'll just look round the shelves before I go, Dan. I want to buy a birthday present for Jake. I'll see you tomorrow, won't I? The party, remember.' And then I looked at Lily who stood there, watching me. Impulsively, I said, 'Thank you for what you did, Lily. And even if I decide not to publish, you'll know that you did the right thing.' I paused, then added, 'And I apologise for the things I said. I was feeling very unhappy.'

She nodded, started to pick up a newspaper and fold it, and said with what I thought was friendliness in her voice, 'I apologise too, Carla. I didn't understand how you were feeling.'

That made me think a bit more deeply. She hadn't meant me any harm; in fact, she had hoped to help me out of my sadness. Quickly, I said the first thing that came into my mind. 'Lily, I do hope you'll come to the party I'm having tomorrow. It's a celebration of May Day. Perhaps you'll come with Dan?'

Surprise spread over her lovely face, and then she reached out a hand and touched my shoulder. Her smile was warm and friendly. 'I should love to come! Thank you so much.'

I knew then that I had misjudged her, and was glad to think I might have made a new friend.

Dan was busy with customers, so I looked at Lily and asked quickly, 'Where are the gardening books, please? I'd like to look at a few.'

She directed me to the shelf marked Gardens, and I smiled my thanks, and then started looking at the titles of the books on the shelf in front of me. But my thoughts were too busy to concentrate on what Jake might like. All I could think of was what Dan had said — that he loved me; and a warm, wonderful certainty spread through me that I loved him back. I knew that our contract of love was real, and waiting for us to enjoy.

Finally I was able to switch my thoughts back to Jake's birthday present, and in the next few minutes I had found it: *Growing a Vegetable Garden.* I smiled to myself. Surely Jake would find this interesting and helpful. I took it to the counter where Dan was dealing with a customer, and waited until he was free to deal with me.

He gave me a small, deep smile that made my heart zing, and I felt emboldened to ask him a very important question. While Jake's book was wrapped and being paid for, I said, 'Dan, the publisher wants to give the series a new name, you said. Please — tell me what it would be?'

He came out from behind the counter and put his arms about me, looking deeply into my eyes and smiling. 'A lovely title, Carla — they want to call it *The Chosen Child.*'

19

What a morning, I thought when I woke up the next day. It was early, with the misty sunshine trying to push its way through my curtains. I took a deep breath of pure joy, and then, feeling my excitement mount, quickly got up and got dressed. I wanted to see the garden before anyone came to disturb its early-morning serenity.

Blackbirds were foraging around the flowerbeds and lawn, and as I made my way up to Jake's allotment I thought I heard a beautiful piping song — and yes, there was a thrush singing on the top branch of the old oak tree. I stood and listened, enthralled by nature's quiet beauty, and I felt a wave of gratitude spread through me. For I was able this morning to dispel some of my fears. Here I was, in the old house I had always loved, just as I did now, with Aunt Jem's presence cheering me on whenever my emotions threatened to overtake me.

The amazing knowledge that Dan loved me, as I loved him, was a warm glow that suffused my body. As I looked down at the sprouting seeds and tall vegetables in Jake's patch, it came to me that I was in the right place. And this was the right day to bring everything together. Or so I hoped. Could I give Dan the one word he was waiting for?

May Day. Smiling, I retraced my steps until I found myself beside the wall of the house, looking into the frail white, scarlet-touched flowers of the thorn tree. I stroked one small flower and said, 'Your day. I do hope you enjoy it.' And then, grinning at such romantic words but knowing they were heartfelt, I went indoors to have some breakfast.

The telephone rang while I was eating toast and marmalade. 'Carla, love — are you all right? I'm afraid it was all rather disturbing yesterday.' Dan's voice was soft and gentle, and I knew I must be honest with him. I finished my mouthful.

'Dearest Dan, how sweet of you to ring. Yes, as you say, things were a bit over-whelming yesterday, and I still haven't really decided what to do about the book. But perhaps when today is all over … '

'The great day. Don't wear yourself out, will you? Lily and I will be over as soon as the shop closes, and I'll help with whatever you want to do. I think you said a bonfire?'

'Yes; we have to celebrate the end of winter, and ask the sun to keep shining for a bit longer!' I giggled and added, 'It's all old-time ideas and thoughts, but I'm sure we'll please the dear old tree with our celebration. And I'll have Jake here, and Annie coming with her husband, Reg. And Meriel, of course. Oh, and I nearly forgot — Kevin is bringing a cake for Jake's birthday!'

We shared a chuckle, and then I said, 'You must give me time to sort out the last of my problems, dear Dan. And when I see you this evening, I just hope I'll have the answer to everything.'

'Yes, and so do I. So, then, until this

evening. And remember — I love you, Carla.' He ended the call, and I realised had marmalade sticking to my lips.

As I started clearing away my plate and cup, there was a knock on the kitchen door, and a familiar voice asked, 'Can we come in, Carla?'

I knew the voice; it was Jake. So who were the 'we'? I wondered. Then, as I opened the door, I saw Ellie smiling at me. She coloured prettily and then held out a small basket covered with a cloth. 'This is our contribution to the party, Carla.'

'Goodness! How very kind of you, Ellie — and Jake, too. You shouldn't have bothered to do this, you know.'

Jake grinned at me. 'Just that we wanted to thank you for everything you've done for us. It's only a few eats to add to the party.'

Curious, I investigated the contents of the basket: some biscuits, some fruit, and two bars of chocolate. 'What a treat,' I said warmly. 'And Jake, come in for a minute will you? I have something to give you — it's your birthday, isn't it?'

He nodded and looked embarrassed, but he took the wrapped present I held out and said, 'Can I open it now, or should I wait 'til later?'

Ellie dug him in the ribs. 'Now!' she said excitedly. 'I wonder what it is?'

The paper fell away, and his expression as he looked at the title and felt the weight of the book was something I knew I would always remember, especially when he found his better allotment and left Thorn House. There was silence for a couple of seconds, and then he took a long breath and looked at me. 'Thank you,' he said hoarsely, already looking at the first page of the book. 'Wonderful — just what I need, Carla. You're marvellous. First the land, and now this ... ' He leaned forward and pecked my cheek. His voice was husky, and his eyes glowed. 'Can't thank you enough for everything.'

Before I could say another word, I heard footsteps crunching along the path, and Annie appeared, followed by a short, plump man with greying hair carrying two more baskets. One was filled with flowers, and the other showed off Annie's cooking ability: small sausage rolls, so appetising that I could only just stop myself from tasting one. 'Mmm!' I said. 'Looks wonderful, Annie! And good morning, Reg. Come in, do.'

Annie at once took out some of her small bunches of flowers. 'Not as grand as yours, but pretty, aren't they?'

They certainly were: pale pink and white little daisies, and a drift of vivid blue forget-me-nots, all done up with tiny bright green leaves. Anne put them in a jug, along with the others that Meriel and I had made, sniffed them, and then grinned at me. 'Well, say what you like, Carla, but I like mine best!'

Then Reg cut in. 'Never mind the flowers. Talked about a bonfire, didn't you, Miss Marshall? Well, I know a little copse with lots of dead branches. I'll go along, see what I can find, and bring it back. Got a bonfire place, have you?' He turned and looked out of the door, saw Jake and Ellie heading for the allotment, and said with a huge grin, 'Love's young dream, eh? Good luck to them. Well, I'll go and ask the boy where he puts the rubbish — that'll be the place.'

Annie put her sausage rolls in the fridge and then looked at me. 'Shall we get out all the eats now? Enough to keep us busy until lunchtime, and then Reg and I must go home. He'll bring the cider barrel later, when the party starts.'

She got out bread rolls, butter and cheese, and then started looking through a cupboard for the chutney. Finally she looked at me, her old eyes twinkling. 'Been outside, have you? You gotta bathe your face in the early morning dew, and then say nice things to the tree. You know it's a lucky tree, don't you? So you gotta go out there and wish. I'll see to all this, maid. Go on, then!'

Half-embarrassed at my romantic thoughts, I went outside and stood close to the thorn tree. 'I know you're a bringer of luck, good old May tree,' I said. 'So please, bring me the luck I know I want so badly. You know how I feel about my adoption, I'm sure. You've been here longer than all of the people who have lived in this house — and they all had problems of some sort, I don't doubt. I want to resolve all mine: the book being published, loving Dan, and finally being able to put aside my silly feelings about my adoption. Please, May tree, do your magic, for all of us who love to come to Thorn House.' I leaned closer and felt a thorn pricking my hand as I raised it to stroke one small flower, and then felt able to do anything. For just that one moment, I guessed happily that the old tree had heard and was trying to reassure me. Yes, there would some magic before the day was done.

And then I saw Jake, his wheelbarrow full of small branches, followed by Reg, who was pulling along a couple of heavy bits of dead wood. Behind them came Ellie, her basket filled with small twigs for kindling. It was all starting to happen, I told myself, and then I let the excitement and happiness grow as I thought what I must do next.

Lunch was rather like a noisy picnic, with Annie and Reg insisting they must go home as she'd left something in the oven, and Jake and Ellie sharing home-made soup and big chunks of bread and cheese. I let them chatter, and realised that Jake was lucky to have this charming, clever girl growing so fond of him. A good pair, I thought, to build a small business.

When he was finished eating, Jake said, 'I'll get the old newspapers from the back of the shed — they'll start the bonfire when you're ready, Carla.'

When I'm ready. I went upstairs with one important thought in my mind. This was the moment to sort out my memories, and to decide on my future. I walked silently into every room upstairs: the box room, the second bedroom, the small porch room where I did the ironing, and then Aunt Jem's room — now mine. It welcomed me, and for a moment I was aware that Aunt Jem had left something behind her that was precious and should be enjoyed. It came to me in a flash. Her love for her chosen child.

It was easy to find her old Memory Box and take it downstairs, where I put it on the kitchen table and looked again at its contents. Bits of jewellery, not worth much, but pretty if you liked dangling earrings and that sort of thing. American nylons. Then the letters — just a bundle of scrappy, scribbled paper. And finally, of course, the little suede bag with the aquamarine brooch inside it. I sat beside the table, thinking, and before too long the answer came. I knew just what I must do with all of them. But then the old clock on the wall struck another hour, and so, with the brooch in my hand, I closed the box and went upstairs. It was time to put on my new party dress.

I knew I looked right for a party. The plain, rather simple dress suited me, and the brooch on one shoulder did all the rest. Brushing my hair until it shone, seeing the smile in my eyes, and feeling excitement growing inside me, I went down to the kitchen to find Meriel on the doorstep.

'A cup of tea, please, Carla,' she

gasped. 'Just come back from an auction where the bidding got so high I thought I would explode.'

I switched on the kettle and smiled at her. 'Did you get what you wanted?'

'Yes.' The one word helped her to relax, and soon she was smiling over the table and drinking her tea as if it were a miraculous cure-all. 'But now, let's think about your party. Have you got the bonfire ready?'

'Jake's doing it. And Annie's Reg will soon be back with his bow saw to cut up the huge branches. You can help me with the food, Meriel, please. I'm making some soup so that we can have it outside in mugs as we watch the fire go down.'

'Mmm. And what about some potatoes in the ashes? Good idea?'

'Great,' I said. 'I'll get some ready.'

We worked together until everything was prepared. Then Meriel, giving me a long look, said, 'Carla, you look prettier, and happier, than I've ever seen you before. Things looking up, are they? I do hope so.'

I touched the brooch on my shoulder and smiled back. 'Let's thank the May tree for its magic, shall we?'

'Magic? Well, of course, you're right.'

Then Reg knocked on the door. 'Done the branches,' he said. 'Time to get the old fire going, isn't it? Would you like to come and supervise, Miss Marshall?'

I gave a last stir to the soup, put the potatoes into a small basket, and followed him out into the garden. I felt it was waiting, ready for the most important part — the bonfire; and with a huge smile on my face, I watched the two men piling wood on the crumpled newspapers bundled in the rubbish site.

Annie took posy after posy out of the big basket she carried, and we all smiled, took one, and somehow attached it to our clothes. Annie's cracked voice rose as she finally cast a tiny bunch onto the fire. 'Come back, sun!' she shouted. 'We need you all the time. Bring warmth and flowers and crops for the farmers.'

There were footsteps behind us, and Kev appeared, wheeling a strangely wrapped contraption which he presented to Jake. He was grinning as he said, 'Happy birthday, lad. And don't say I never approve of what you're trying to do.' Clearly perplexed, Jake tore the wrapping paper off the new wheelbarrow, and happiness instantly brimmed in his eyes. Kev put an arm around his brother, and his grin grew even bigger as we all cheered.

The fire came to life without any trouble: first the paper, then Ellie's small kindling, and finally the huge branches. We all stood around, watching; and as I looked at the intent faces beside me, I realised that this fire really was a part of country life. I could see interest, amusement, and a certain hopefulness on everyone's face, and I was sure it was all reflected on my own.

As the flames grew higher, the heat mounted, and we all took a step back. It was a lovely time. Meriel took my hand, pulling me closer to her. 'Magic,' she murmured, and I nodded.

And then the real magic happened — Dan was beside me, his arms suddenly around me. I turned so that I could look into his smiling face. 'My lovely Carla. So it's all happening then, just as you hoped.'

His arms were warm, strong, and inviting. Laughing, I looked around the little audience and wished I could kiss him; but that would come later, I knew. When the ritual was over, the fire had died, and everyone had gone home, Dan and I would be alone. But for now, I was the hostess and must see that my guests had all they wanted.

The soup was a great success, and so were the potatoes. 'Lovely, Miss Marshall,' Reg enthused. 'Annie, you must get this recipe.'

Annie frowned and turned away from him, though then she looked at me and nodded, muttering between chuckles, 'Men and their stomachs ...'

A voice behind me made me turn, and there was Lily. 'I brought you a little something,' she said, smiling. 'Because I made you unhappy, and because I'm so glad to be here tonight with you.'

It was a small, much-used book:

Folklore About May Day. I leaned forward and put a kiss on her cheek. 'I shall love reading it, thank you very much, Lily. And now you and Dan must have posies.'

Smiling, she tucked the small bunch into the collar of her blouse, and I watched Dan putting his into his jacket buttonhole. While they all turned again to watch the fire, he took the opportunity to pull me closer, and then bent, kissing first my cheek, and then gently my mouth.

Standing apart again, he looked at the brooch on my shoulder and said, 'Carla, my love, how beautiful you look this evening. And the brooch is just right.'

I nodded. 'Yes, it is lovely. And today, Dan, I've decided what I'm going to do with it.'

He frowned slightly. 'And all the other problems?'

But I didn't answer, for suddenly the fire erupted into shining sparks which fell all around us. We stepped away — all of us except for Jake, who grinned and said, 'Time to do the leaping, isn't? I'll go first and show you how. Here, Ellie, take my hand and we'll do it together.'

We all took deep breaths as the couple jumped through the dying fire. And then, one by one, we did the same. With the heat licking up and sparks having to be brushed off skirts, we cried out in excitement and delight.

20

The fire was still glowing even as the sun slipped down behind the trees. We gathered in the kitchen, and Kev's amazing cake was cut as I made coffee. The little room seemed full of people, busy with chatter and laughter. We ate slices of the chocolate sponge covered with raspberries dipped into chocolate, and congratulated Kev on his expertise.

Eventually, it was time for everyone to go home. Kev offered Ellie a lift back to town, Jake pushed his bicycle into the back of the old white van, and they drove off with cheery honks and waves. Annie pulled Reg away from what was left in the cider barrel, and the couple walked down the path arguing about something; but Annie gave me a last wave, and I saw a glint of pleasure in her eyes. Meriel suggested that she drive Lily home, and this was accepted because we all knew that Dan would stay in Thorn House for a while yet, to spend some quiet time with me after the riotous evening celebrations.

And so, finally, as the last guest left and closed the door behind them, Dan and I were alone. His arms enfolded me within their warmth and strength, and I thought what a marvellous evening this had been.

'At last,' he said, almost in a whisper, and drew me close. We kissed, and then stood looking at each other, and I felt the last dregs of my problems die away for good.

I smiled at him and said, 'The one word you wanted, dearest Dan, is yes.'

'You mean you'd like your aunt's book to be published, and you're pleased about it? No more trouble about the adoption story?'

I took a deep breath, and found that it helped me to put everything into perspective. 'Yes,' I said. 'I want the three books to go out to readers, and I no longer mind that the heroine is an adopted child, as I am. Oh Dan, today I've realised what love is all about. Mine for you, yours for me, and dear Aunt Jem's for the child she chose. How could I ever have been so puzzled and foolish, I wonder.'

He laughed into my eyes. 'Because you are what you are — a feeling, emotional, loving person who's had more than her fair share of fears. But you say it's all over now, my darling? Are you quite sure?'

I drew away from him and said, 'Yes, I am, Dan. And to prove it, I have a last duty to carry out. Please stay there for a moment.'

I went to the cupboard where the Memory Box was hidden, got it out, and put it on the table. He looked at me in surprise, but I smiled as I took out everything that was in the box.

'Time to put all these things into the past,' I told him. 'This pretty jewellery is to go to Annie, who has a daughter who loves such things. And the nylons ... perhaps Annie will wear them when she wants to pretty herself up. And now the letters.' I opened the little bundle and pushed them across the table for him to look at. He skimmed through them, read the names, and then looked at me again.

'Love letters,' he said quietly. 'From people who had been in love; women who wanted children, and the story of how you came to live at Thorn House. What are going to do with them, my darling?'

I got up, the letters in my hand. 'I'm going to burn them, Dan,' I said. 'They're just bits of the past, and we should be living in the present. So — come with me, will you?'

Outside, the garden was shadowy, with a sliver of a new moon dipping through the incoming evening clouds. We stood by the ashes of the fire, and Dan, finding a stick, poked the glowing sparks. Briefly they flamed, accepting the letters and quickly burning them. They were gone.

Dan and I drew close again, and we smiled at each other. 'But surely there's something else you have to decide, Carla?' he said, and his warm fingers touched the aquamarine brooch on my shoulder. We both looked at it. It caught a brief glow of moonlight, and looked so beautiful that for a moment I wondered if my decision to get rid of it was the right one.

We walked slowly back to the house, stopping by the thorn tree. And then I realised that yes, I was right in what I planned to do with this lovely thing. I said, 'I shall ask Meriel to put it into a jewellery sale, and then donate the proceeds to an adoption society. Do you think that's a good idea, Dan?'

He simply nodded, put his arms around me, and whispered, 'Yes.'

In the doorway we stood still, looking at the thorn tree, and in my case thanking it for tonight's undoubted touch of magic. Then I went into the kitchen and turned to look at Dan, waiting. I knew that what I waited for would be the last, most important touch of magic in this amazing day.

He didn't disappoint me. Another step and he was beside me, as I turned to close and lock the door. His voice was low and amused as he said, 'Not going to turn me out into the cold night, are you, my lovely?'

I laughed as I headed for the staircase.

'Well, there is an ancient camp bed in the box room — you could try that.'

We went up the stairs together, and I silently thanked Aunt Jem and Thorn House for bringing me safely home.

We do hope that you have enjoyed reading this large print book.

Did you know that all of our titles are available for purchase?

We publish a wide range of high quality large print books including:
Romances, Mysteries, Classics
General Fiction
Non Fiction and Westerns

Special interest titles available in large print are:
The Little Oxford Dictionary
Music Book, Song Book
Hymn Book, Service Book

Also available from us courtesy of Oxford University Press:
Young Readers' Dictionary
(large print edition)
Young Readers' Thesaurus
(large print edition)

For further information or a free brochure, please contact us at:
Ulverscroft Large Print Books Ltd.,
The Green, Bradgate Road, Anstey,
Leicester, LE7 7FU, England.
Tel: (00 44) **0116 236 4325**
Fax: (00 44) **0116 234 0205**

*Other titles in the
Linford Romance Library:*

SUMMER'S DREAM

Jean M. Long

Talented designer Juliet Croft is devastated when the company she works for closes. She takes a temporary job at the Linden Manor Hotel, but soon hears rumours that the business is in financial difficulties — and suspects that Sheldon's, a rival company, is involved. During her work, she renews her friendship with Scott, a former colleague. At the same time, she must cope with her growing feelings for Martin Glover, the hotel manager. Trouble is, he's already taken . . .

SEEING SHADOWS

Susan Udy

Lexie Brookes is busy running her hairdressing salon and wondering what to do about her cooling relationship with her partner, Danny. When the jewellery shop next door is broken into via her own premises, the owner — the wealthy and infuriatingly arrogant Bruno Cavendish — blames her for his losses. Then Danny disappears, and Lexie is suddenly targeted by a mysterious stalker. To add to the turmoil, Bruno appears to be attracted to her, and she finds herself equally drawn to him . . .

A DATE WITH ROMANCE

Toni Anders

Refusing to live in the shadow of her father, a famous TV chef, Lauren Tate runs her own cake shop with her best friend, Daisy. Having been unlucky in love, Lauren pours her energy into her business — until she meets her handsome new neighbour, Jake, who is keen to strike up a friendship with her. Will Lauren decide to take him up on the offer? Then Daisy has an accident, and announces she'll be following her partner to America once she has healed — leaving Lauren with some difficult choices . . .